Once ag... att... ... ... of Clint's personality.

And she knew that the feelings surfacing now were the same ones that had plagued her so long ago.

She was falling for Clint Fletcher all over again.

Was she an idiot? How could a heart work so independently of a mind?

Nadine looked heavenward. *Why, Lord? Why am I falling for this man? Please take away these feelings. Please.*

She stopped, waiting for a still, small voice to guide her, to steer her heart away from Clint Fletcher.

But she heard nothing....

Books by Carolyne Aarsen

Love Inspired

Homecoming #24
Ever Faithful #33
A Bride at Last #51

CAROLYNE AARSEN

has been writing stories almost as long as she has been reading them, and has wanted to write a book for most of her life. When she could finally write "the end" on her first, she realized, to her dismay, that it wasn't. Three rewrites later it turned into a book that was finally marketable. What she learned along the way was to write a story that was true to what she believed and the kind of books she liked to read.

Her writing stems from her life's experiences. Living in a tiny cabin with five children in remote British Columbia, opening their home to numerous foster children, helping her husband build the house they now live in, working with their cattle on their ranch in northern Alberta—all become fodder for yet more stories to come.

What Carolyne wants to do with her writing is show that our Christian life is a growing, changing relationship with God and a constant fight with our own weakness. Thankfully, God keeps taking us back.

A Bride At Last
Carolyne Aarsen

Published by Steeple Hill Books™

STEEPLE HILL BOOKS

Steeple
Hill™

ISBN 0-373-87051-5

A BRIDE AT LAST

Copyright © 1999 by Carolyne Aarsen

Printed in U.S.A.

We do not know what we ought to pray for, but the
Spirit himself intercedes for us....
—*Romans* 8:26

This one is for Jesse, Cheyanne, Fern and Amiel, my dear children, who have had to make do with a part-time mother when deadlines loom. Thanks, kids, for your patience and understanding.

Chapter One

Nadine folded the letter she had just read and carefully slipped it into the envelope, as if any quick movement might jar and rearrange the disturbing words. She laid the envelope on her desk and ran her thumb along its sharp edge. As she weighed the information the letter held, her thoughts were intermingled questions and prayers.

She leaned back in her chair and drew her hands over her face. *Is this it, Lord?* she prayed. *Are we finally going to find out the truth?*

Nadine, along with her mother and sisters, had speculated on the mysterious circumstances surrounding her father Jake Laidlaw's death over six years before. It was midwinter and he had been working for Skyline Contractors as a tree faller. The only information his grieving widow and daughters had received was the official incident report the company had released, which stated that Jake had died because of his own carelessness.

But Nadine and her family knew better than anyone Jake's penchant for safety, the care with which he had performed his work. Although they didn't believe the company, they had never found out more.

Until now.

The anonymous letter gave out no specific information, but hinted at knowledge of the events surrounding her father's death.

From the day of the accident Nadine and her mother had been determined to find out the truth. Nadine's sisters, Sabrina and Leslie, had lost interest after a few years.

This letter was the first break Nadine had had in six years. Her only regret was that she wouldn't be able to share a breakthrough with her mother.

Six months ago after a protracted battle with Lou Gehrig's disease, Brenda Laidlaw had died. Her determined nature could not help her conquer her illness any more than it could help her find out what had really happened to her husband.

Nadine picked up the envelope and slipped it into her backpack. Her workday as editor of the *Derwin Times* was over.

She caught her suede bomber jacket off the coatrack against the wall and slipped it over her bulky knit sweater. Fall clothes, she thought, flipping her shoulder-length hair out of the collar and retying it into a ponytail. Last week she'd worn a T-shirt. And then the temperature had suddenly dropped.

She glanced with dismay at the bits of straw still clinging to her corduroy pants and picked the pieces off, dropping them in the overflowing trash can under her desk.

The afternoon had been spent out in farmers' fields taking harvest pictures. She had never been able to stay as neat and tidy as her sisters. Growing up, she was always the one with dirt on her elbows and rips in her jeans.

"Hey, Naddy, you still hanging around here?" Donna, her friend and the office manager of the weekly newspaper, stopped in the doorway, her arms full of computer printouts. Donna blew her copper-colored bangs out of her eyes and leaned tiredly in the doorway.

"Actually I'm heading home." Nadine smiled up at her friend. "What's with the papers? Some light evening reading?"

"Circulation records. Clint wants to bring some of the ex-subscribers back into the fold." Donna plopped the stack of papers on Nadine's desk, then dropped into one of the chairs across from Nadine's desk.

"You look tired yourself," Nadine said, noticing the faint shadows beneath Donna's usually bright green eyes.

"The big boss is a different kind of general manager than Dory ever was," said Donna with a sigh. "I just have to get up to speed, that's all."

"Excuse me, can I come in?" The deep voice coming from the doorway made Nadine and Donna both jump. Donna threw Nadine a look of dismay, and turned to face Clint Fletcher.

"I was just coming with the printouts, Clint."

"That's fine, Donna. I'm in no hurry." Clint stepped into the room, his presence suddenly dominating it. The collar of his crisp gray shirt was cinched by a burgundy tie, his thick brown hair was attractively tousled, his face, as usual, impassive. His hazel eyes were on Nadine. "I received this with my mail and mistakenly opened it. I wasn't aware it was addressed to you personally until I started reading it. I apologize."

Nadine took the envelope. "Thanks, Fletcher. I'm sure you were discreet," she said, unable to keep the flippant tone out of her voice. Clint always managed to keep her on edge, and sarcasm was her favorite defense.

Clint only nodded. "I was also wondering if I could see you in my office first thing tomorrow morning?"

"Another editorial mini-summit?" Nadine laughed nervously, uncomfortable with the somber tone of his voice.

"You might say that," he said, his tone cryptic, his expression still serious. "Just bring those papers to my office whenever it's convenient, Donna."

Ever since Clint had started, the usual routines at the paper had been rearranged, changed and turned end over end. Dory Strepchuk, the previous general manager, favored a looser editorial style and had pretty much let Nadine, as editor, make a lot of her own decisions.

Clint, however, had made it quite clear that he wanted to be involved in the major editorial decisions of not only the *Derwin Times,* but also its sister papers, the *Eastbar Echo* and the *Riverview Leader.*

"I wonder if our esteemed boss knows that I have a name?" Nadine said after he left. "You get called a name," she said to Donna. "Wally has a name. He even called our ex-reporter Bradley Nichols by name. But somehow he studiously manages to avoid calling me anything."

Donna shrugged. "Doesn't help that you always call him Fletcher."

"He's been Fletcher to me for the past nine years. From the first day he went out with my older sister," Nadine groused, "to the last." She hefted her knapsack onto her back, still flustered by Clint's visit and the seriousness in his voice when he had spoken of their meeting tomorrow. "And what's with the clothes?" she huffed. "He never used to dress like that when he lived in Derwin before."

"He's not like you, wearing some of the same clothes he wore in grade twelve."

"My mother made me this sweater," protested Nadine, glancing down at the bulky cream sweater.

"And the pants?"

Nadine simply shrugged. She disliked shopping for clothes. Once in a while her sisters would come home and drag her off to a store. They would laugh together, trying on clothes and having fun coaxing each other to buy new things. Nadine would take her new outfits home, hang them in the closet and pull on her old faithful jeans or cords. Usually, she dressed up only for church.

"It wouldn't destroy your tough editor image to dress up once in a while yourself," continued Donna. "Put on a skirt. Show off your legs."

"Give it a rest, Donna. I'll just stick with pants. Makes it easier for climbing up on tractors and fences, anyhow."

"And fending guys off..." Donna let the sentence trail off as she straightened the stack of papers on the desk.

"Been there, done that," Nadine replied, fishing in her pocket for her car keys.

"Four years ago, I might add. And I don't think your heart was ever in that relationship," Donna admonished her. "A boyfriend wouldn't really cramp your style, you know."

"Don't start," Nadine begged. "You sound just like my grandmother. I thought I had a few days' reprieve from her matchmaking. My sister Sabrina's not been feeling well since she had Megan. With any luck, Grandma will stay there and drive Sabrina crazy for at least a week."

"Is Grandma *that* bad?"

"Not really. I'd just prefer to live alone, I guess."

"I know your grandmother. She won't leave until you have a boyfriend or until you very firmly say,

'Danielle Laidlaw, time for you to go back to Calgary.' And since you won't do either, you're stuck with her.'' Donna settled in a chair across from Nadine, her legs stretched out in front of her. "So my advice to you is get a boyfriend.''

Nadine rolled her eyes. "Sure. I'll just head down to the nearest 'guy' store and pick one up.''

"Well, there's lots of eligible guys in Derwin.''

"Besides the ones Grandma keeps dragging home?''

Donna winked. "Our dreamy boss, for one.''

Nadine skewered Donna with an angry gaze. "Give me a break.''

Donna pursed her lips as she looked Nadine over. "I think you would make a good couple.''

Nadine ignored the soft sting of Donna's words. She had grown up a dark brunette between two tall, slender blondes. She loved her sisters dearly, but while they loved going out, she preferred to stay home. But that Clint Fletcher, whom she had secretly admired from afar, had gone out with her older sister and flirted with the younger had been harder to deal with. "I'm not his type,'' she grumbled.

"You never give yourself enough credit.'' Donna studied her friend, her head tilted to one side.

"I like myself just fine. But I'm not his type. End of story.''

"Okay, no Clint. But what are you going to do about Grandma?''

''I should just tell her to move out,'' Nadine said after a moment.

Donna laughed. ''That sweet, tiny woman will just bat those blue eyes, smile at you and hand you a plate of cookies. And then she'll tell you that she's having yet another single, totally unsuitable man over for supper.'' Donna straightened. ''I think the best way to get Grandma to go home is to make up a boyfriend who conveniently doesn't live in Derwin.''

''Like I could pull that off,'' replied Nadine. ''I don't have a good enough memory to lie.''

''The Lord helps those who help themselves.'' Donna grinned at her friend.

''That's not even in the Bible.''

''So I'm an office manager, not a theologian.'' Donna pushed herself to her feet, pulling the stack of papers off Nadine's desk. ''I'd better get going. I promised my family real food for supper tonight. Want to join us?''

''Thanks, but tonight I'm going to enjoy being in an empty apartment, put on some music and eat *two* bowls of cereal for supper.''

Donna pulled a face as they walked out of Nadine's office and down the hall. ''Sounds like a big night.'' Donna stopped outside Clint's office door. ''See you tomorrow, wild thing.''

''That's what they call me,'' Nadine teased back as she tossed her friend a wave.

Nadine stepped outside, into the late-afternoon warmth of September. In spite of the shared laughter with Donna, a feeling of melancholy washed over her.

It was a glorious fall day, and with a sigh she pocketed her keys. She didn't feel like driving home. It would take just twenty minutes to walk and she had to come straight back to the office anyhow. She could leave her car parked at the office overnight and she knew it wouldn't be harmed.

Nadine ambled down the tree-lined sidewalks of her hometown, hands in the pockets of her pants, her jacket hanging open and her knapsack slung over one shoulder. She scuffed her running shoes through the layer of leaves lying on the sidewalk.

It's a beautiful world, Lord, Nadine thought, squinting upward. The sharp blue Alberta sky stretched up and away, contrasting sharply with the bright orange and yellow leaves of the aspen trees lining the street. Derwin was the proverbial small prairie town. It had the requisite grain elevators solidly planted along the railroad track, streets in the older part of town sitting at right angles to it disregarding true north and south. Nadine had been born and raised in Derwin. In typical small-town-girl fashion, she had planned her getaway ever since high school started. Her plans had been to take journalism and photography courses and find a job with a city newspaper or small magazine and work her way up. She'd had two semesters of school and the city and a boyfriend. Then her mother became ill, Dory offered her a job and Nadine gave up all three.

For five years Brenda Laidlaw had fought Lou

Gehrig's disease. When the disease was first diagnosed, the doctor had given her only three years, but he hadn't counted on Brenda Laidlaw's temperament or persistence. She vowed she wouldn't rest until she found out what had happened to her husband. But she couldn't win this losing battle. In spite of her prayers, God had other plans for her. And in spite of Nadine's sorrow, her mother's death had also been a relief. The saddest part of the disease was that while Brenda's body failed her, her mind still understood all that happened around her. The death of her mother six months ago, while not unexpected, had plunged Nadine into a deep grief that could still rise up unexpectedly, the feelings still fresh and intense.

Nadine drew in a deep breath of the fall air, a heaviness of heart accompanying thoughts of her mother. Must be the season, she thought. Fall always brought a pensive air.

She shook her head as she turned the corner to her apartment, willing the mood away. At least she could look forward to a quiet evening at home. Whistling softly, she approached her house, then caught sight of a small red car parked in front of the two-story, redbrick walk-up.

Grandma.

Nadine glanced upward as if to question God, shook her head and unlocked one of the double glass front doors. She walked down the hall to her suite and sent out a prayer for patience as she opened the unlocked door and stepped inside. The mouthwatering smell of peanut butter chocolate chip cookies drifted down from the kitchen into the entrance and began an ominous growling in her stomach, reminding Nadine that she had skipped lunch.

With a groan she dropped her knapsack on the table in the side entrance, toed her runners off her feet and stepped around the corner into the kitchen.

A tiny lady, no more than five feet high, soft gray hair cropped short, was perched on a stool in the small U-shaped kitchen area, singing softly as she rolled cookies, laying them in precise rows on the baking sheet beside her.

Nadine pulled a face and cleared her throat, announcing her entrance.

The sprite whirled around, and the strains of "Nearer My God to Thee" faded away as she beamed at her granddaughter. "Naddy! You're home." Grandma jumped down from the stool, walked over and lifted her head for a kiss.

"Hi, Grandma." *What are you doing back here, Grandma? How long are you staying here, Grandma?*

"Sabrina was doing just fine and didn't really need my help with the baby," Grandma explained, "so I thought I would come back here."

Nadine's heart sank as her silent questions were answered. She felt frustrated with her sister's recuperative ability.

"From the look of the place, I'm not a moment too soon." Grandma shook her head.

Nadine ignored the reprimand in her voice and

glanced around the kitchen for any changes her grandmother might have wrought. Sure enough, She had moved the kitchen table into the corner again. She claimed it made the kitchen roomier. But Nadine liked it directly under the chandelier. It shed a better light, with no shadows.

The timer rang out and Grandma went back to her cookies. She pulled open the oven door to take out the next batch. "When I saw all those piled-up cereal bowls in the sink, I knew I shouldn't have left."

"Cold cereal is a well-balanced meal," huffed Nadine, shoving the high-backed wooden chairs back under the table with one knee. "It says so on all the commercials."

Danielle rolled the cookie balls vigorously. "Tonight it's just good, warm food for you. So go wash up. I'll have supper on the table in a few winks."

"You're only staying for a while longer, right?" Nadine asked, remembering past promises blithely broken by her grandma.

Grandma threw an innocent look over her shoulder. "I'll stay as long as you need me."

Nadine held that guileless stare a moment as if to decipher what that meant, but Grandma only winked at her. Nadine straightened the last chair and headed down the hall to the bathroom.

She glanced around the bathroom and wrinkled her nose. This morning she had been rushed and had dropped her clothes and towels on the floor. Now the bathroom taps sparkled and clean peach-colored towels hung on the towel bar, with a gray facecloth the same shade as the walls lying in a perfect triangle across them. The bathtub shone and a clean rug lay in front of both the sink and the tub.

As she tugged a brush through her thick hair she thought about her dear, sweet, interfering grandma.

When Nadine's mother had been in the first stages of Lou Gehrig's disease, Danielle Laidlaw had moved in to help Nadine and her sisters take care of Brenda and the housekeeping. When Brenda was transferred to the hospital, Grandma stayed on. Sabrina and Leslie, Nadine's sisters, got married and moved out. Grandma didn't. Danielle was perfectly capable of living on her own, but preferred to rent her house out and stay to help Nadine.

Grandma "helped" Nadine by cleaning, baking, organizing and inviting "suitable" men over for supper. She thought it was better for Nadine to be involved in church, and regularly volunteered Nadine's services.

Nadine got a break from Grandma only when an anxiously placed call to one of her sympathetic sisters would result in a sham mission for Grandma Laidlaw. From time to time, Grandma would promise Nadine that someday soon she would move back home.

But that day never came, Grandma always insisting that poor Naddy still needed her.

The biggest problem was that poor Naddy was still single.

Not that poor Naddy didn't have a chance. She'd dated Jack for slightly more than a year when they

got engaged. Then Nadine's mother got sick and
Nadine wanted to move back to Derwin, but Jack
didn't. Nadine knew she had to come home. When
Jack failed to understand, she knew she had to break
up with him.

Nadine pulled a face at herself in the mirror.
Maybe if she'd been an alluring blonde, he might
have waited, he might even have come to Derwin
to be with her.

As always, she was critical of the upward tilt of
her own brown eyes, the heaviness of her hair, the
fullness of her jaw. It was, as her grandma was wont
to say when trying to console her, an interesting
face.

Nadine ran the tap and washed her interesting face
and hands.

She opened the door to the room that doubled as
bedroom and office and breathed a sigh of relief.
The old rolltop desk still overflowed with papers,
magazines still lay in various piles around it.
Grandma hadn't invaded her domain. So far.

After changing, she stepped out of the room and
with a furtive glance down the short hall, opened
the door to the spare bedroom across from hers. In
''Grandma's room'' the suitcases were put away and
the Bible lay on the bedside table. Framed family
pictures marched across the dresser.

It looked as if Grandma never planned to go.

Nadine squared her shoulders and walked deter-
minedly down the hallway. She would step into the
kitchen, take a deep breath and say…

"Sugar or honey in your tea?" Grandma set a steaming mug on the table just as Nadine marched into the kitchen. Her determined step faltered as Grandma caught her by the arm and led her toward a chair. "Supper's ready."

Nadine opened her mouth to speak, but Grandma had already turned her back and begun putting the food on the plates. Nadine sighed as Grandma set them down on the ironed tablecloth, then settled into a chair and beamed at her granddaughter. "It's nice to be back again. I missed you, Naddy." She held out her hand. "Do you want to pray, or shall I?"

"You can." Nadine was afraid that she would voice aloud her own questions to God about her grandmother's presence in her home.

Danielle asked for peace and protection and a blessing on the food. When she was finished she began eating with a vigor that never ceased to surprise Nadine. "So, what happened while I was gone?" Danielle asked.

"Not much," Nadine replied, thinking back over the quiet of the past few days.

As they ate, Nadine told her grandmother about the articles she was working on.

"I thought maybe that nice young man David might have called," Danielle said with a lilt on her tone. "I can't remember his last name. We met him at the grocery store."

"David Branscome is unemployed by choice and lives at home. Hardly dating material."

Danielle appeared unfazed. "A good woman can make a huge difference to a man."

"David already has a good woman. His mother." Nadine finished off the food on her plate and laid her utensils on it. "That was delicious, Grandma. Mind if I pass on dessert? I've got some work to do."

"You work all day—surely you don't have to work all night?" Danielle asked.

"It's nothing really important. I just want to get it done before tomorrow," Nadine said vaguely. She rose and picked up her dishes.

Nadine was hesitant to mention the letter she had received. Jake was also Danielle's son, and she was loath to raise any false hope that they might finally solve the mystery surrounding his death.

"I need to look over some information about Skyline," she added carefully.

Danielle turned to Nadine, her expression sorrowful. "Oh, honey, that always makes you so angry. Don't you have anything better to do?"

"They just received some government grants that are questionable," she said, keeping her tone light. Nadine took her dishes to the counter and set them down. "It won't take long."

She left the room before guilt over her evasive answers overwhelmed her. *I could never fib well,* she thought as she walked down the hall.

Chapter Two

Nadine closed the door to her bedroom and leaned against it, thinking of the mysterious letter and all it portended.

She had a letter that promised some answers and possibly hard proof she could bring to Skyline. Once again Nadine wondered at God's will in all of this. Why had the letter come now, after all this time?

With a short sigh, she walked over to her desk and switched on the computer. While it was booting up, she pulled the envelope out of her knapsack and reread the letter.

Dear Ms. Laidlaw,
I've read your pieces about Skyline in the paper. I know you don't have any love for Skyline. Neither do I. You are right. I need to talk to you about your father. In person. I have

some information that I think you can use against Skyline. I'll call.

It wasn't signed, and there was no return address. It had been dropped off at the office while Nadine was out and, according to Sharlene, their receptionist, it was lying on her desk when she returned from lunch.

Nadine refolded the letter and pulled out the other one that Clint had given her just before she left the office.

She skimmed it quickly. An official-looking letter announced the opening of a new farm equipment dealership in Derwin. The cover letter was addressed to her personally, and Nadine glanced over it, as well. It asked about advertising rates and the writer wondered if the newspaper would be willing to give him some coverage on opening day. Nadine glanced at the return address, but didn't recognize the name. She would have Donna contact the business and give them the information they needed.

For now she had work to do.

Nadine turned back to her computer and called up Skyline's file, where she kept copies of all the letters she had written to the company's management, as well as various government departments dealing with industrial safety. The correspondence had netted her a few polite responses couched in the vague language of bureaucrats. These replies had been scanned back into the computer and saved on file.

Nadine opened them all up and read each one in chronological order to refresh her memory. Rereading the letters reminded her once again of what she and her family had lost. A loving, hardworking father whose sincere faith in a loving Savior had tempered their mother's harsher view of God. A father who listened with a sympathetic ear, who fixed temperamental bicycles and vehicles for daughters too busy to realize how fortunate they were to have been raised by such a man.

Nadine leaned her elbow on her desk, recalling pictures of Jake Laidlaw striding up the walk in the late evening smelling of diesel and sawdust, swinging up each of his daughters in his strong arms and laughing at their squeals, pulling Brenda away from the stove, spinning her around and enveloping her in a tight, warm hug. Her father whistling as he organized his tools, readying them for the next day's work. Her parents had never made a lot of money, but they had achieved a measure of contentment that often eluded people with much more. Jake was convinced of God's ability to care for them. Unfortunately that conviction created a measure of lassez-faire over his personal dealings with banks and insurance companies, who were less forgiving.

Because her father was considered a contract worker, he'd had no company pension plan and no private life insurance. Neither was the loan against the house insured. The pittance paid out by Worker's Compensation had barely paid expenses. Brenda Laidlaw had worked for barely a year as a cashier in the local grocery store before her illness made her housebound. The house was sold and the family moved into an apartment in the same building where Nadine now lived.

Nadine pulled herself back to the present and looked around the room. When her sisters had got married and moved out, she and Grandma and her mother had moved to this first-floor suite that was more easily accessible for Brenda, then confined to a wheelchair.

Now, with her mother gone, the apartment was too large for a single girl. She had her eye on a smaller, newer apartment complex. But moving away felt as if she was breaking the last tie with her mother.

And you've got Grandma, she reminded herself with a sigh. Moving to a smaller place would probably be the best way to get Grandma to go back to her own place but it seemed an unkind and disrespectful solution. When it came to facing down Danielle, too many memories intervened.

Echoes of her grandmother reading devotions to her mother, singing while she carefully gave Brenda a sponge bath and fed her, lovingly wiping her mother's mouth as Brenda's control decreased.

Grandma's service to her and her mother had been a blessing at the time, but now it seemed to entwine itself around her. Nadine didn't know how to shake free of Grandma's gentle grip of generosity without feeling ungrateful and unloving.

Nadine rolled her shoulders, rubbed her eyes and turned back to the computer screen. Grandma and a new apartment would have to wait.

A gentle knock on the door interrupted her.

"What is it, Grandma?" she asked, frowning in concentration.

"We have company," Danielle announced loudly.

Nadine glanced over her shoulder at her grandmother, who stood in the open doorway smiling at her. "Who is it?" she whispered.

"Don't you want to do your hair?" Danielle whispered back.

"No," Nadine replied irritably. She would have preferred to stay in her room, but it wasn't in her to be so rude to their unnamed visitor.

Nadine followed Danielle down the short hall, through the kitchen into the living room. The pewter table lamps shed a soft light on the room. Nadine couldn't help but feel a measure of pride in the fawn-colored leather couch with matching chair. Burnished pine-and-brass coffee table and end tables complemented the warm tones of the leather. She had made the plaid valances that hung by tabs from the pewter curtain rods and the matching throw pillows herself.

A man stood with his back to her. He turned as they came into the room and Nadine bit back a sigh.

"Nadine, I'm sure you remember Patrick Quinn. Didn't he used to live four houses down from us when we lived on 55th?"

Nadine smiled at Patrick, praying the fake expression she pasted on masked her seething thoughts. She tried to suppress memories of Patrick as a boy—selfish, overbearing and constantly teasing her.

Other than rudely turning around and returning to her office, which would be most un-Christlike and unforgiving, she had little choice but to sit down and try to make some kind of small talk.

The talk turned out to be *very* small, with Grandma and Nadine asking Patrick polite questions about where he worked and lived. Patrick had changed little, Nadine reflected, or possibly he had become even more boring.

After a while Nadine had to do something. Stretching her leg under the coffee table, she gave her grandmother a gentle nudge.

Danielle didn't even flinch.

"Our Nadine is quite the little cook..." Grandma continued, ignoring Nadine's next push, delivered with a little more force.

"I'm neither little nor a good cook," interrupted Nadine. She gave her grandmother a warning look, then glanced back at Patrick. "Grandma would love me to be more domestic, but for me, gourmet cooking means putting brown instead of white sugar on my cereal."

Grandma didn't miss a beat. "She's such a joker, our Nadine."

Thankfully, at ten o'clock Patrick rose and excused himself. He thanked Danielle and Nadine for a lovely visit and, with a playful smile at Nadine, left.

Danielle turned to Nadine. "He's such a nice boy. Don't you think?"

"If you like that type," Nadine said dryly.

"He wanted to see you again. I can tell." Danielle bent over to put the mugs on the tray and then, as the clock struck, straightened. "Goodness, Nadine. You had better get to bed. I'll clean up. You need your sleep."

And with that, Danielle bustled off to the kitchen.

Nadine shook her head. She had to do something about Danielle, or her meddling grandmother was going to take over her life.

She yawned a jaw-cracking yawn and glanced at her watch. But not tonight.

It was still early morning when Clint Fletcher pulled open the door to his office. He smiled as he looked around the neat room. The sun had just come up, and lit the eastern sky outside his window, illuminating the space with a gentle light.

His office, he thought with a proprietary air. During the years he'd worked in the city for one of the large newspapers, he had been lucky to have his own desk in a large, crowded newsroom. Even then he would often come back from an assignment to find it appropriated by a colleague whose computer was down.

Now, not only did he have his own desk, he had his own phone, his own door and an element of privacy. He set his briefcase down on his desk and walked to the window. His uncle Dory had occupied

the office farther down the hall. It was larger, but
when Clint had taken over the papers, he'd also
moved to this office. He preferred the view. He liked
to look up from his desk and see people in the park
across the street or walking past the office busy with
their town errands.

It had been Nadine's office before he came, and
he was sure there was a certain resentment over that,
he thought as he idly watched the play of wind in
the trees arching over the street. He still didn't know
what he had done to create Nadine's guarded looks,
the touchy attitude. Nor did he understand why she
still called him Fletcher.

She had always called him that. His first memory
of her was of brown eyes watching him warily from
a porch swing as he came to their home to pick up
her older sister. She had been reading a book, and
when he came up the walk she put it down and
demanded to know who he was. After that he was
simply addressed as "Fletcher." It became a challenge to coax a smile out of her, to get her to speak
more than a few words.

He had gone to church with Sabrina as much to
see how Nadine would react as to please his girl-
friend. She wasn't impressed. Nor was she impressed when he started showing up occasionally at
the Bible studies on Wednesday nights. He had more
reasons to attend than just to impress Nadine, but he
hadn't been ready to admit his seeking to anyone.

Nadine was indifferent and Clint's ego was pro-
voked. He wasn't used to having girls indifferent to

him. Consequently he began to show up earlier for
dates, seeking out Nadine, talking to her, drawing
her out. He found he spent more time talking to
Nadine about serious issues while he waited for her
sister than he did with Sabrina. He enjoyed their
time together and thought Nadine did, too. He knew
it was time to break up with Sabrina when he found
himself loath to leave Nadine when it was time to
leave the house with her sister.

He had gone out with a number of girls when he
left Derwin, but none of them challenged him intel-
lectually the way Nadine had. None of them had her
appeal. Nor did they ever keep him at arm's length
as she did.

Now she was working for him, and it seemed that
the intervening years, with all the sadness they had
brought to her life, had once again put a prickly shell
of defensiveness around her. He had returned to
Derwin with the hope of seeing her again, raising
their relationship to another level, but each of his
overtures had been rebuffed. After his first weeks
here, he held back, sensing that Nadine was still
dealing with the grief of her mother's death.

Their relationship had become a cordial business
one, but in the past few weeks he had begun to see
glimpses of the Nadine he'd always loved.

Clint shook his head at his own thoughts. Regardless of his feelings for her, he had a job to do.

He walked back to his desk and, snapping open
his briefcase, pulled out the letter he had received
yesterday from Skyline Contractors. Correction, he

thought. Skyline Contractors' lawyers. He didn't look forward to discussing it with Nadine.

"I made pancakes, Nadine," said Grandma as Nadine came into the kitchen.

"Pass, Grandma. I'm not in the mood for a big breakfast."

"You never are," complained Danielle, looking up from the newspaper.

Nadine tugged open the refrigerator door and pulled out a carton of yogurt, a container of milk and an apple. She juggled the three items, carefully set them on the table, then dropped into a chair. Last week's newspaper was spread out on the table. Grandma was reading the first section, so Nadine grabbed the other.

She opened the pages, skimming over the stories that she knew almost by rote, stopping at her kindergarten feature.

She thought she had done some pretty effective work with the pictures she had taken. She had pasted them in a montage of children's faces, eager, expectant and excited. The mix had energy and exuberance suited to the first day of a new venture. It was the kind of picture she knew parents cut out to put in their child's scrapbook.

"Listen to this item from the 'Court Docket,'" Grandma said, her voice scandalized. "Holly Maitfield fined for allowing her dog to roam the neighborhood unleashed. Again." She clucked anxiously.

"They're going to put that poor mutt in the pound one day."

"They'll have to catch him first," murmured Nadine, skimming over the text opposite her feature. Halfway through she sighed in frustration. Another typing error. She had missed that one. Clint would be annoyed. Maybe that's what he wanted to see her about this morning.

"That's an amazing picture," commented Grandma, leaning over to look at the paper.

Nadine couldn't help but glow. In this line of work people commented more often on what the reporter had done wrong, rather than right. Her grandma's compliment warmed her. "Thanks, Grandma. I had a lot of fun with this feature." She smoothed the picture with a proprietary air and turned it so her grandma could see it better. Nadine was about to turn the page when her grandmother stilled her hand.

"Wait a minute, I want to read 'About Town.'" Danielle held her hand on the paper while she read the bits of local gossip gleaned from a variety of sources for this regular feature. Nadine never read it. She couldn't be bothered. But Grandma read it faithfully. If she read it in "About Town," it had to be true.

Nadine finished her breakfast and prepared herself to face down Danielle Laidlaw.

"Grandma, I need to talk to you."

Danielle blinked, put down her fork and crossed

her hands on the table in front of her. "This sounds serious."

"It is. I like organizing my own social life, choosing my own friends. I don't think you need to invite suitable young men over for tea."

"I didn't really invite Patrick. He asked himself over. He wanted to see you," Danielle insisted.

Nadine stared across the table at her grandmother, ignoring the remark. "I don't want you inviting anyone over for tea, okay, Grandma?"

Grandma Laidlaw smiled back at her, unperturbed by Nadine's pique. "I'm sorry, Nadine," she continued, her tone contrite. "I'm sorry you feel like I'm interfering in your life. I just want you to be happy, settled. That's all." She got up and took the teapot off the stove. "Do you want a cup of tea yet, honey? It's your favorite kind. I got it in that store on the corner. The one with that good-looking young cashier."

"No, thanks." Nadine frowned, her anger fading. But somehow, she knew her grandma had done it again. Taken the wind out of her sails and then changed tack.

"Well, then, you probably should get going. Make sure you're home on time tonight. We've got company for supper."

Nadine stopped, her frustration trying to find an outlet, trying to find words. "Who?" she sputtered, angry with her own reaction, angry that she couldn't seem to find the right words to make her grandmother understand.

"I know you said no more interfering, but I had invited Dr. McCormack for supper tonight a couple of days ago. I can't change that now. He works in the new clinic I've been visiting," Grandma said quickly.

Nadine's resolve from the previous evening returned with a vengeance. Grandma just didn't get it. If Nadine couldn't come up with her own boyfriend it looked as if she was going to spend the rest of her life across the supper table from potential suitors as her grandmother recounted her accomplishments, going back to kindergarten. Well, two could play that game.

"I won't be home," she said firmly.

Grandma frowned. "Why not? You're not working, are you?"

She wasn't and she knew she had to do some fast work to avoid a repeat of last night and many other nights. "Actually…" What, what? She actually was going to do…what? Her mind flew over the possibilities and then latched on to one in desperation. "I have a date." She smiled in triumph.

"A date? With who?"

Oh, brother. Who? "Uh…Trace."

Grandma frowned again. "I've never heard of this Trace fellow. What kind of a name is that? What is his last name?"

This was getting harder. She didn't even know where she had pulled the name Trace from. It had just popped into her mind. Now he needed a last name, to boot. "Trace…Bennet," she quickly added. Nice name, respectable name, she thought to herself. "He's a great guy. I met him a couple of months ago at the Agribition in Edmonton when I was doing a story on the farm family of the year." She rinsed off her bowl, unable to look her grandmother in the eye, and bit her lip to stop the flow of drivel mixed with absolute fibs.

"You never told me about this." Grandma sounded hurt.

Nadine shrugged nonchalantly, ignoring a stab of guilt. She reminded herself of the stories Grandma had spun to Patrick and the fact that Grandma had told her Dr. McCormack was coming over only seconds after Nadine had specifically asked her not to invite prospective boyfriends.

"I'm meeting him in Eastbar," Nadine said, turning with a smile at her grandmother. "I have to do a review on a new movie showing there." Time to quit, Nadine, she thought.

Grandma sat back in her chair, almost pouting. "That's so too bad. I was really hoping for you to meet Dr. McCormack. He's quite good-looking."

"Well." Nadine lifted her shoulders in a shrug. "Sorry, but I can't break a date with Trace." She brushed a quick kiss on her grandmother's cheek. "So long," she added, straightening.

Grandma caught her hand and squeezed it as Nadine straightened. "Do you like this man?"

Nadine almost relented at the sight of her grandmother's worried expression. Grandma really did only mean the best, she thought. But she steeled herself, knowing that Grandma's strongest ammunition was her concern and consideration. "We're just getting to know each other, Grandma. These things take time."

"Well, then, it shouldn't matter if I ask someone else over, should it?"

She just wouldn't give up, thought Nadine incredulously, holding her grandmother's gaze, determined not to back down. "I have a boyfriend now, Grandma. You don't have to worry about me. You never had to." And with that she turned and left before she was forced to make up any more lies.

Trace Bennet, Trace Bennett, she repeated to herself as she walked out the door. I've got to remember that name! She stepped out and hurried down the walk, her guilt hanging over her like a dark cloud.

Chapter Three

Clint stepped out of his office into the airy, spacious foyer. It still held that new smell of paint and carpet glue. He had ordered the renovations as soon as he took over, knocking out one wall and putting a curved, chest-high divider that acted as reception desk. The room was done up in shades of cream and hunter green. The staff referred to it as the restaurant, but most agreed that it made the office look more professional and inviting.

Sharlene was already at her desk, answering the phone and trying to bring a measure of order to the office.

"When Nadine comes, can you tell her I'd like to see her right away?" he instructed the receptionist.

Sharlene nodded, and just as he was about to go back to his office, the door opened with a jangle of chimes and Nadine stepped into the room, rubbing her hands. A flow of cold air accompanied her and as she looked up, she stopped, glancing at Clint, then sharply away.

Clint couldn't stop the nudge of disappointment at her reaction. It was no different than usual, but it still bothered him.

He cleared his throat. "When you've got a few minutes, Nadine, I'd like to see you."

"Okay. I'll be there right away." Without giving him another glance, Nadine walked to Sharlene's desk and leaned on the divider. "Any mail for me?"

"Just these. And a letter with no return address."

Nadine caught the letter, turned it over and shoved it in her ever-present knapsack. "I'll get the others when I come back."

Finally she turned back to Clint, her head back as if challenging him. Clint bit back a sigh. Why did he even bother with this woman? She would never let down her guard with him. She would never come to care for him as he did for her. But as he caught her eyes, he saw pain and weariness behind the light of challenge, and he felt the impulse to hold her, comfort her.

He would just have to be patient. After all, didn't the Bible tell us that love is patient?

"You wanted to see me right away?" she said.

"If you have a moment."

Nadine shrugged. "Better get me now before the phone starts ringing."

Clint ushered her into his office, but before she

sat down he offered her a cup of coffee, which she declined.

"You mean I don't even get to show you what a sensitive, caring guy I am?" he joked in an attempt to alleviate the mood.

She looked up quickly, a smile teasing the corners of her mouth. Clint smiled back as he sat down.

"I know what kind of man you are," she said quietly.

That stopped him. Things were looking up. And he needed all the optimism he could muster.

"So what did you want to talk to me about?"

Clint took a breath, trying to find the right words, reminding himself that he was the general manager and protecting the newspaper was his first priority, not furthering his personal relationship with his editor. He rested his arms on his desk. "I wanted to ask you about an article on Skyline Contractors that I found in the computer archives. It was under your byline, but obviously not ready for press yet. Is it news?"

Nadine's face hardened and Clint sighed. "I got some information from a former employee about some discrepancies in their accident reports…" she said slowly.

"Who verified it?"

"A former employee who used to drive Cat for them. Of course, the operative words are 'used to.' He heard a few things he shouldn't have, repeated them to me and now he, too, is a former employee."

She leaned forward. "Trust me, Clint. This is a story and it's good."

"I don't want you to write the story."

"If you want to pull rank on me, Clint, that's fine. But before we go any further, I want to talk to the editors of other papers in the organization. They have as much a stake in this fight as we do. You know they'll take my part. I have to run this story."

"Skyline will kill themselves in the long run. Do you really think they need our help?"

Nadine held his gaze. "Well, it seems to me to be a good cause, so I say why not?"

Clint knew she was right, but he also knew that he had to make sure she wasn't setting out stories just for the sake of antagonizing a company that had their lawyer's number on speed dial. "Why not? Because this time they might take us to court, for one reason." He pulled back his frustration. The newspaper business was a tough go and he was thankful for the loyal readership and the comfortable living he was making. He wanted to keep it that way.

Nadine shrugged. "Their lawyers make a lot of noise, but they always back down when we respond."

"Have you talked to anyone who works for Skyline now?" he persisted.

"C'mon Clint. The management likes me as much as you do."

Her comment hit him, hard. "What do you mean by that?"

Nadine shrugged, not deigning to reply, looking anywhere but at him.

He got up from his desk, puzzled that she should think that, and wondering if maybe that wasn't the key, the true reason she kept herself at such a distance from him. "Why would you think I dislike you?"

As he came to stand beside her, she stood as well, looking up at him, her dark eyes wide.

He remembered the smile she had given him just a few moments ago, wondering what she would do if he touched her cheek, if he ran his fingers through her hair as he always wanted to, if he…

"WordCo is on line two for you, Mr. Fletcher." Sharlene's voice on the intercom pierced the heavy atmosphere. Clint blinked, Nadine took a step back.

"Well, I'd better get going. You look pretty busy," she said with a short laugh. She picked up her knapsack, slung it over her shoulder and left.

Clint turned back to the phone, frustrated and angry at the intrusion. He punched the button and answered curtly, "Hello."

"Hey, Clint. Don Pederson here. How are you?"

Clint sighed at Don's fake friendliness. Sounds like a salesman, he thought, even though Don wasn't selling. He was buying, and what he wanted to buy was Clint's small string of newspapers.

"You actually did it?" Donna stabbed her French fry in the ketchup with a grin. "My pure, unadulterated friend actually fibbed to her grandmother?"

Nadine blew her breath out in a sigh and leaned her elbows on the pink tabletop of the Downtown Deli. "I had to. First it's Patrick Quinn last night for tea, then Dr. McCormack tonight for supper."

"Dr. McCormack?" Donna grimaced and shook her head. "He's about fifteen years older than us and, while I think bald men can be very attractive, on him it's not." She leaned forward. "So what name did you give this pretend guy?"

Nadine closed her eyes in concentration. She had to write his name down somewhere or she was going to blow it completely. "Trace Bennet."

Donna pulled her mouth down. "Sounds like a country and western singer. What does he look like?"

"Goodness, Donna. He's fake."

"Knowing your grandma, she's going to phone me asking about all the gory details. We're going to have to do a biography on this guy." Donna laughed. "We need hair color, eye color..." She pursed her lips, thinking. "Job, place of employment."

"Don't bother." Nadine waved a hand over the table in dismissal. "I just blurted it out this morning because I was angry, and wanted to keep her off my back. There's no getting around it. I'm just going to have to go home and tell her, 'Grandma, move out.'"

"Why don't you let her stay and you move out?"

"Don't tempt me." Nadine pursed her lips as she looked out of the café's window, which faced the newspaper office. Some days it seemed as if her life stretched ahead of her like a prairie road. Predictable and the same. Not that she needed high adventure, she added to herself. She was content here in Derwin. She enjoyed her work, enjoyed her life. She just wished she had someone she could share it with. She recalled her morning meeting with Clint. The way he'd looked at her just before the phone call. For a moment it had seemed as if something was building between them. Nadine shook her head, dismissing the notion. Just wishful thinking. She wasn't his type.

She glanced up at the clock. "Yikes. I've got to get going. I promised Fletcher I'd get pictures of the rodeo."

"And you've got to get ready for a big date," Donna teased.

"Right." Nadine paid the bill, tossed a wave at Donna and left.

Donna watched her go. She knew her friend wouldn't be able to face down dear little Grandma Laidlaw. Nadine might be able to poke holes in Clint Fletcher's composure and fast-talk her way out of awkward interviewing situations, but family situations were another story. There Nadine always avoided rocking the boat.

And now Nadine was making up fake boyfriends in a bid to keep her grandmother off her back. But Donna knew, if Nadine had her way, she wouldn't keep up the sham very long. A very principled person was her friend Nadine.

Well, Donna was going to give things a little push and help Nadine persuade Grandma that Nadine was just fine. She grinned. Donna knew Grandma Laidlaw and knew exactly how to go about it.

The movie was a dud. Nadine struggled through it, scribbled a few comments and as soon as the credits began to roll, fled the theater. Outside, the streetlights had just come on, competing with the setting sun. The evening still held vestiges of the day's warmth, and beyond the town Nadine could hear the faint drone of combines and tractors harvesting the fields.

She knew she should have been home, working over some stories for the next issue, but she had told Grandma she would be out tonight.

If Grandma found out she'd gone alone to the film, she would start her matchmaking all over again. It was frustrating, not to mention slightly humiliating. Before Jack, Nadine had never gone out with many guys, just a few casual dates. But nothing had ever clicked. And after she broke up with Jack she ended up back in Derwin, taking care of her mother.

Nadine loved her job, loved where she lived. The time she had spent going to school in the city had cured her of any desire to work and live there. But the other reality was staying in Derwin, slowly seeing her friends move away or marry the boy they had gone out with since high school.

Nadine hadn't dated much in high school, and had

never really minded that much. Until Clint Fletcher. How acutely she'd felt the lack of a boyfriend once Clint began dating her older sister. How awkward and boring she'd felt watching Sabrina make him laugh, when all Nadine could do was debate the most ponderous issues. How it had hurt to watch him leave the house with Sabrina for their dates, even though she would never admit that she had been attracted to Clint from the first moment she'd seen him.

When Clint came back to Derwin, it was as if her life had suddenly turned back. Old emotions melded with new ones and it seemed that each time she and Clint met it was with wary cynicism on her part and an impassive seriousness on his. Nadine was left to wonder at the irony of life and puzzle out what exactly God planned for hers.

Nadine squinted up at the darkening sky, past the streetlights of Eastbar. The crescent moon hung in the sky above her. A few of the brighter stars showed themselves in the blue-black sky. Beyond these lay more stars, more constellations, other galaxies. She stared upward, aware of what a small part of creation she really was. Just a small speck in the whole cosmos that God had created. She kept busy with the Mission Committee at the church. She went to the Wednesday-evening Bible study when she wasn't on assignment. Each Christmas she joined the choir to sing at the nursing homes and the city jail. She enjoyed her work, but lately, when she came home, she felt as if something was missing. Did she really have a right to expect more?

She knew she didn't, but once in a while a deep yearning overrode her desire to be alone. A yearning to have someone waiting at home besides an older grandmother who didn't really need her.

Her parents had had that, thought Nadine, giving an empty can a tinny kick. She remembered her big, burly father, his warm hugs, smelling of diesel and sawdust. When his work required it, he would stay in the bush for a week. This was in the days when hand harvesting was more common, before mechanical machines took a week to chomp their way through what would have been a full winter's work. Nadine remembered how he used to grab her mother around her waist and swing her off the floor, singing loudly. Her mother would laugh, wrap her arms around his neck and sing along. The waiting was over. The man of the house had returned. All was well.

Now, instead of life amidst her parents and sisters, all she had at home was her dear, meddling grandmother.

Nadine thought back to her conversation with Donna and wondered if she could put Grandma off the scent with her fake boyfriend. She knew beyond a doubt that she didn't have the resources to maintain the fib. This "date" would have to be a one-time thing, she mused, pulling out the keys to her car. She was surprised she'd gotten this far.

Nadine glanced at her watch. Too early to go home. It would have to be coffee at the Derwin Inn.

"I'll just have a coffee, Katya." Nadine smiled up at the waitress, who nodded and tucked her order pad back into her apron.

Nadine sipped the hot brew, wondering how long she dared draw this out. It was only 10:30 p.m. Grandma would still be up.

She looked around the coffee shop of the Derwin Inn, a place known more for its food than its coffee. The Derwin Inn had new owners since the last time she'd been here. Skylights had been installed framed by boxes of ivy, leaves cascading downward, echoed by umbrella plants strategically located to break up the space. The room was painted a soft yellow, and the windows had scarves of ivory and green draped across them. It looked more like a spacious living room than a coffee shop.

Nadine tried to imagine hefty truckers sitting at the delicate, glass-topped tables and smiled at the picture.

"Share the joke?" The deep voice beside her broke into her thoughts. She jumped, her hand hitting her coffee cup.

She grabbed a handful of napkins and, still mopping up, turned to face Clint Fletcher. "You scared me out of my wits," she accused him, her heart pounding.

"Now, that conjures up an interesting image. Nadine without her wits," he said dryly, still towering over her, his one hand in the pocket of his pants, the other resting on the table.

Clint hesitated a moment, then pulled out a chair. ''Mind if I join you?''

She tried not to let his height intimidate her, tried not to notice how broad his shoulders looked covered by a suit coat. Tried to ignore the increase in her heartbeat at the sight of him.

She shrugged in answer. He could take that how he liked, but deep down, she felt a faint hope that he would stay, then berated herself for still feeling attracted to him after all these years. Feelings he clearly had never shared. Clint Fletcher was her boss and nothing more.

''What story are you covering that keeps you out so late?'' he asked as he sat down.

She fiddled with her cup. ''I caught the movie in Eastbar, which was dreadful, and thought I'd kill some time before I go home.''

''I take it the review won't be favorable.'' Clint folded his hands on the table and leaned forward.

''Not likely.'' Nadine laughed and sat back against her chair. ''I'll probably have Evan Grimshaw accusing me of trying to put him out of business again.''

''Who did you go with?'' asked Clint, a little too casually, as he smoothed down his tie.

''No one you'd know,'' she replied evasively.

Clint nodded and for a moment Nadine was tempted to drop Trace Bennet's name. But she knew

Clint with his quick, incisive questions would catch her out, and that would look worse.

"So does your grandmother still live with you?" he asked conversationally.

Nadine traced her finger through the circles of moisture the mug had left behind on the table. "Yes, still," she replied with a sigh. "She's a dear old lady, but I do wish she'd go visit my other sisters and bother them for a while."

A moment of silence hung between them. Clint cleared his throat. "How are your sisters?" he asked hesitantly.

Nadine caught the tone in his voice and, looking up at him, caught a melancholy expression on his face. She wondered if he still missed Sabrina. For a moment she felt sorry for the usually self-possessed Clint Fletcher. She knew exactly what it felt like to be the one spurned, the one left behind. "Sabrina had her first child a few months ago and has just returned to work. Leslie is expecting as well, but she's quitting her job before the baby is born."

"She always was a homebody. Just like you." Clint smiled at Nadine, his expression softening. Then, just as suddenly, the moment was gone. He stood and straightened the cuffs of his shirt and once again became her boss. "Well, I'd better be off. I have a busy day tomorrow."

"'Court Docket.'" Nadine grinned at him. "A little bit of a comedown for our esteemed G.M. to have to cover for Wally."

He paused and for a heartbeat looked as if he was

going to say something else. Then, lifting a shoulder, he turned and left.

Nadine looked down at her half-full coffee cup. Suddenly she felt very alone. A lonely alone, she thought as she set the cup down and dropped a few quarters on the table for Katya, grimacing at her watch.

Grandma would still be up and she would have to answer some tough questions about her "date."

Chapter Four

"C'mon Nadine," Grandma called down the hall. "We're going to be late for church."

Nadine stifled a wave of impatience with her dear grandma as she straightened a cream-colored sweater over her rust wool skirt and tugged on the elastic holding her hair. It snapped against her hand and her hair slid loose.

"Are you coming?" Grandma called again.

Nadine glanced at the clock and, with a frustrated sigh, grabbed her purse from the bed and slung it over her shoulder. She stopped at the bathroom long enough to quickly brush her hair and grimace at yet another reflection of herself. She felt self-conscious wearing her hair down. A ponytail was far easier, but she could find no elastics in the bathroom, either. Down it would have to stay, she thought.

"Nadine." Grandma's voice was uncharacteristically sharp, and Nadine threw the brush into the drawer. "Coming, coming," she muttered as she ran down the hallway.

Grandma waited in the porch, her mouth pursed in disapproval. "What took you so long?" she grumbled.

Nadine caught her car keys from the little peg-board hanging by the back door. Without deigning to reply to her grandma, she stepped out on the porch, then strode down the sidewalk to her car.

"You are certainly not in a Sunday mood today," Grandma chided as she stepped into the vehicle.

"Sorry, Grandma," Nadine said automatically as she started up the car and backed it onto the street. "But after you cleaned up the other night, I couldn't find my clothes."

"I'm sure you didn't want a mess." Grandma folded her hands over the small purse she had on her lap. Staring primly ahead, she remained quiet for the rest of the trip.

Church was full again. Over the summer, attendance had waxed and waned, with people leaving for holidays, but now the children were back in school, the harvest was in full swing and the congregation was back to full strength.

"You just go on ahead, Nadine. There's someone I want to talk to." Grandma gave Nadine a gentle push into the sanctuary. Nadine frowned at her, wondering what she was scheming now, but when she saw an elderly woman wave toward Danielle, she relaxed.

"Don't wait too long, Grandma. Church is pretty full," she warned.

"Don't worry about me," Grandma chirped as she walked over to her friend. Nadine shook her head and let the usher show her to an empty spot.

Nadine dropped into the pew and scanned the bulletin that came with the order of worship. It was filled with the usual announcements. Church school was starting again, catechism classes, Ladies' Society and choir. Nadine made note of the choir practice and began reading a handout from the Mission Committee.

Out of the corner of her eye she saw Grandma stop beside the pew, glancing backward down the aisle.

Without looking up, Nadine scooted over for Grandma and her friend, turning the page of the bulletin as she did so.

"Come sit with us," she heard her grandmother say. Nadine glanced up idly to see who her grandma was talking to. Her heart sank.

Clint Fletcher stood in the aisle, one hand on the pew in front of them, the other in the pocket of his trench coat. Underneath he wore a tailored navy suit, a white shirt and a patterned tie in shades of deep gold and russet. Nadine felt her heart lift at the sight of him.

"Here Nadine. Let Mr. Fletcher sit between us." As Grandma sat down, she nudged Nadine over. Nadine silently fumed, but could do nothing without creating a scene. So she merely moved aside so Clint could sit between them.

Nadine picked up the bulletin, trying to ignore both her grandma and the tall figure seated beside her. It couldn't be done. Clint's presence exerted a force that she couldn't ignore. So she thought it would be better to do as she always did and face him head-on, hoping he wouldn't read anything into Grandma's little machinations.

"So, what brings my esteemed boss to church this morning?" she said, forcing a teasing grin.

He glanced sidelong at her. "Same thing that brought you."

Nadine couldn't resist. "You have a nagging grandma, too?"

Clint smiled and shook his head. "No. A nagging conscience."

Nadine was taken aback at his quiet admission. No quick reply came to mind, so she picked up her reading where she had left off. But she couldn't forget what he had said, and during the service she cast sidelong glances at him. His expression was, as usual, serious. He sang along with the hymns, obviously familiar with them. As he listened to the minister Nadine recognized that firm-jaw look that came over his face when he absorbed some particularly important idea.

Nadine was surprised at his intensity. Clint had accompanied Sabrina to church, but she had never gotten the impression from him that his attendance meant anything. She had challenged him once on it and had received a sarcastic remark. But he didn't look sarcastic right now.

When the offering was passed, he took the plate, dropped in an envelope and handed it to her. He didn't let go, however. Nadine looked up at him, puzzled.

"Your hair looks nice like that," he said quietly.

Nadine raised her eyebrows, almost dropping the plate. Flustered, she handed it to the person beside her, forgetting to put in her own contribution. She tried to stifle the flush that warmed her throat and crept up her cheeks.

Compliments from Clint Fletcher? That was something she had no defense for.

Nadine felt more and more uncomfortable sitting beside her boss. She would manage to bring her mind back to the sermon, but then he would shift his weight, move his long legs or brush her arm with his elbow and she would have to start all over again. Periodically she caught a spicy hint of aftershave. Mentally apologizing to God, she took a deep breath, pulled out a notepad from her purse and focused her entire attention on the minister. The reporter in her made it easier to remember sermons when she took notes.

When the congregation rose for the last song, she finally risked a sidelong glance at him. He looked down at her from his considerable height, and Nadine looked hurriedly away, feeling even more confused.

What did he want from her? Why was he here?

She was relieved when the organist and pianist began the postlude. It wasn't often that Clint could throw her for a loop, but his presence in church beside her and his unexpected compliment did.

As she made her way down the crowded aisle to the exit, she glanced over her shoulder. Clint had been waylaid by Mr. and Mrs. Enright, the owners of an auction business that advertised frequently in the *Derwin Times*. He was smiling now, his features relaxed. Nadine's step faltered as she saw him grin, then laugh. He was attractive enough when he was serious. Smiling, he became irresistible.

Nadine shook her head at her own reaction. With a forced shrug, she continued out to her car. Grandma already sat waiting, and Nadine slipped in behind the wheel.

"By the way, Nadine." She smiled, turning guileless blue eyes to her granddaughter. "Mr. Fletcher is coming over for lunch."

"What?" Nadine almost dropped her car keys. "But, Grandma..."

"I know what you said," Grandma interjected, "but he invited himself over. What could I do?" she asked innocently. "I always thought he was too smart for Sabrina. Leslie flirted outrageously with him, but I think he secretly liked you the best," Danielle continued, undaunted by Nadine's expression.

"He kept that secret well," Nadine said dryly, looking away. "I sure never got that impression."

"Maybe because you were always so snippy to

him. I'm sure he'd have spent more time with you
if you'd softened a little.''

"May I remind you it was Sabrina he went out
with. Clint never looked twice at me," Nadine remarked, pulling her keys out of her purse.

"He has eyes for you, Nadine. I can tell,"
Grandma persisted.

Nadine shook her head. "Grandma, I already
have a boyfriend."

"Yes, I know. I keep forgetting." Danielle smiled
at Nadine. "I'd like to meet him."

Nadine glanced at her grandmother, but made no
reply as she pulled out of the parking lot.

"What are you doing in the kitchen?" Grandma
caught Nadine by the arm, frowning up at her. "You
go talk to Clint."

Nadine neatly laid out the cheese slices, quelling
her irritation. "You invited him, you talk to him,"
she whispered back.

But Grandma would not be swayed. "You pour
Clint some coffee," she said loudly, smiling at Nadine. "I'll finish up in here."

Nadine counted to ten, grabbed the pot and
marched out of the kitchen. Clint sat on the edge of
the couch. He smiled hesitantly up at Nadine as she
filled his coffee cup. Nadine straightened, still holding the pot. She couldn't help but smile back. Nor
could she help the soft flip of her heart as their eyes
met. It was just like the other morning in his office

when the atmosphere held a hint of a promise of other things to come.

"Lunch is ready," Grandma announced from the kitchen, and once again the mood was broken. Clint picked up his cup, motioning for Nadine to precede him.

After grace was said by Grandma, it was her game. She chatted amiably with Clint, praising her granddaughter, drawing her into the conversation. Nadine felt uncomfortable and embarrassed by Grandma's obvious matchmaking, and was positive that Clint felt the same.

But he gamely answered Grandma's questions, and if Nadine didn't contribute much to the conversation, he didn't seem to mind. However, it was an awkward affair and Nadine silently promised herself that once Clint was gone, she would have it out with her dear grandma. Once and for all.

Thankfully, after dessert and more polite conversation, Clint said he had to hurry off to another appointment. Grandma didn't hide her disappointment, and Nadine was grateful for his tact. He bid them both farewell, and as soon as Nadine closed the door behind him, she turned to face her grandma.

Danielle yawned delicately and glanced at her watch. "I'm tired, Nadine. I think I'll lie down. Can you clean up? Thanks." With that, Grandma walked away.

Nadine watched Danielle close the door to her bedroom. Then she turned to the kitchen full of leftovers and dirty dishes, left to wonder how she had let Grandma finesse her way out of both the dishes and another confrontation.

And wonder why Clint had accepted the invitation.

Monday was the usual deadline chaos—phones ringing, typesetters requesting changes in articles that didn't fit the layout.

A fire came in over the police scanner and Clint ended up running out to cover it. To make room for the fire, Nadine had to scuttle her plans for her harvest article taking up the top half of the page.

"C'mon, Clint. I can't finish the layout for that page until I get your story," one of the typesetters groused.

Nadine walked past Clint, who sat, head bent over the keyboard of a computer he had taken over. She paused, looking over his shoulder. Clint seldom wrote articles, but since they were still short a reporter, he had offered to cover the story. She remembered all too well how disconcerted she had felt yesterday, first at church, then at her home. She was determined today to get the upper hand once more in their relationship.

"Accident has two *c*'s," she said lightly.

"I'll run the spell-check once I've finished," he muttered.

"If you remember," Nadine said, leaning one hip against the desk, watching him. He looked agitated, a mood she seldom saw overtake the usually self-possessed Clint Fletcher.

"Don't you have some pictures to paste together or cut apart, or something?" he snapped, pausing to loosen his tie, undo his cuffs and roll up his sleeves.

Nadine paused at the sight of his muscular forearms. "Now *this* is a real first," she said, laughing to cover her reaction. "Clint Fletcher loosens his tie!"

Clint frowned at her. "You should be someplace else."

"I have a newspaper to lay out, and I can't until you hand in your copy."

"Well, if you want my copy, you should be anyplace else but right here." He continued frowning at her and, as their eyes met, Nadine felt her heart slow. She blinked, and the moment was lost. She abruptly pushed herself away from his desk.

"Okay. I'll go check on your courthouse notes for the 'Court Docket.'" Nadine left the room, frustrated with her changing emotions.

The day rambled on. Clint got his story done. A few pieces had to be edited, a few photos resized to fit. By late afternoon the bulk of the work was done. Nadine and a typesetter would be at the paper until late evening setting it all out. Tuesday morning the staff of the *Derwin Times* would start all over again on the next edition.

"What are you doing later tonight?" Donna paused by Nadine's office on her way home to her own family. "We're going to rent a couple of movies, and eat greasy hamburgers and popcorn in front of the television. Want to join us?"

Nadine wrinkled her nose, considering. "We'll be done early tonight, but I should go home. I told Grandma I would spend some time with her instead of my imaginary boyfriend."

"And how has she taken to the idea that her granddaughter has a boyfriend?"

Nadine pulled her hands over her face. "She wants to meet Trace."

"Oh-oh."

"Yeah. Big oh-oh. And where am I going to haul up a boyfriend named Trace Bennet?" Nadine shook her head. "I shouldn't have started this business, Donna."

"No. It's definitely a one-way path to ruin and destruction, this fake boyfriend," Donna gibed.

"Don't joke about that, Donna."

"Don't you always tell me to trust? Maybe you should do the same."

"This is completely different. I can't possibly pray that the Lord will miraculously send me a boyfriend to support a lie I told my dear grandmother." She sighed. "I had hoped just the mention of it would be enough."

"Well, go home, sleep on it. Who knows what will happen?" Donna winked at Nadine, leaving her to ponder what to do about a certain Trace Bennet and the consequences of her lie.

Clint leaned back in his chair reading the most recent edition of the *Derwin Times*, taking a moment to appreciate the new leader they were using. It was a struggle to update the fonts, clean out a lot of the deadwood and encourage the reporters to be more creative. Some had resisted change, but others were eager to take a new direction.

He snapped open the paper, skimming the stories, not reading as much as measuring impact. All in all it was a clean, sharp-looking paper that had the potential to win an award this year at the Weekly Newspapers Association convention. It was one of his goals.

Instituting changes had been a struggle, but slowly the editors of all three papers were coming around.

He turned to the editorial section and was immediately confronted with a picture of the one who wasn't.

Nadine Laidlaw.

Clint tilted his head, looking at the grainy picture on the top of her column. Her large eyes stared back at him, her full mouth unsmiling. The picture didn't do her justice. He studied her face wondering as always why Nadine kept him at arm's length. Just won't fall for your irresistible charm, he thought, laughing lightly at his own egotism.

Grandma Laidlaw, however, was always kindness and consideration. And not above a little matchmaking, he thought wryly, remembering her machinations of Sunday. He was pleased to have such a strong ally in his corner, and hoped the time he'd spent with Nadine on Sunday had brought them a few steps closer.

He turned the page to "About Town," giving it a cursory glance. But it was the usual. The name of a town councillor spotted at the golf course during one of the meetings, other well-known people and their goings-on. Local reporter Nadine Laidlaw spotted at the theater in Eastbar with...

"What?" Clint frowned, shaking the paper as if to bring the name into focus. "Who in the world is Trace Bennet?"

He suddenly realized he had spoken aloud, and quickly glanced through the open door to see if Sharlene had noticed. Thankfully, she wasn't at her desk. He looked back at the paper and reread the piece. Was he a boyfriend?

And why was that name so familiar? Maybe Nadine had mentioned it when he'd met her the other day at the Derwin Inn. Thinking back, he remembered she had been evasive about who she'd been with.

He suddenly felt very foolish. She already had a boyfriend, and kept making it clear that she wasn't interested in him. Yet he continued to try.

Sharlene was now at her desk. She looked up and smiled as Nadine walked in. "Hey, Nadine," she heard her call out.

Clint couldn't help the tingle of awareness as he heard Nadine's name. He straightened as she entered the main office area and dropped her knapsack on the reception desk. Clint allowed himself a moment to look at her. She had an athletic build, which appealed to Clint far more than the slenderness of her sisters. Her cheeks were ruddy from the morning air. Her thick, dark hair was pulled back into the ever-present ponytail he remembered so well. As usual, she wore pants.

"Let's see the latest news from the bustling metropolis of Derwin," Nadine said, her grinning face in profile to Clint.

Sharlene slapped a paper into Nadine's outstretched hand, and she laid it out on the counter, eyeing the front page. She glanced Clint's way and, holding up the paper, winked at him. "Nice shot, eh?"

He sauntered over, hands in the pockets of his dress pants holding back his suit coat. "Looks great, Nadine. Good job."

Nadine smiled. "Thanks, my sartorial boss." She turned her gaze back to the paper, flipping the pages just as he had done a few moments ago. Clint could tell by the way her soft brown eyes traveled over the pages that she was looking at them the way he had. Not reading, just checking for overall impression.

He watched her a moment, feeling almost sorry she had pulled her hair back into a ponytail again. Sunday, wearing a dress and with her hair hanging loose on her shoulders, she had looked softer, more approachable. Less the sassy reporter and more womanly.

He let his eyes travel over her face. She had a firm mouth offset by exotic-looking eyes that tilted upward at the corners, accented by narrow eyebrows. Her striking features drew him again and again. He had been attracted to her from the beginning, yet was put off by her prickly manner. But somehow the intervening years had softened her features. Sorrow had granted her an air of vulnerability he was sure she was unaware of.

Nadine seemed to sense his gaze and looked up at him, their eyes meeting. Clint felt once again the spark of awareness he experienced each time their eyes met.

"Cute little piece in 'About Town' on your trip to Eastbar," he gibed, needing to know about this boyfriend.

She frowned and turned to the section. As she read the piece he could tell to the second when her eyes hit her name. A flush shot to her hairline. She swallowed and, without looking at him, slapped the paper shut, caught her knapsack with her other hand and marched down the hallway.

Clint raised one eyebrow in surprise, his curiosity further aroused by Nadine's reaction. Not typical of a woman in love, he thought, feeling a little better. Maybe all was not lost.

"You did this. I know you did," Nadine hissed, shaking the paper in front of her friend's face.

Donna rose and shut the door to her office. "Of course I did," she said. "I know your grandma always reads that section. Doesn't she?"

"But...the paper," Nadine sputtered. "To put it in the newspaper..."

"Oh, c'mon. Most people know it's idle gossip. But your grandma puts as much stock in it as anything she hears from the pulpit on Sunday. I knew if she read it, it would bolster your cause." Donna walked over and patted her friend on the head. "Trust me. It's for the best."

She looked up at Donna and then back at the paper. "So what do I do?"

"Nothing, you ninny. Grandma will read it, believe what you told her, and then she'll move out. Which I might remind you," Donna said, her voice stern, "was the point of this whole exercise."

"But she wants to meet this guy. I have to do something."

"Just hope that this little piece in the paper will be enough. Send her on her way and tell her you'll bring him up for Thanksgiving." Donna sat back on her desk, her arms crossed. "Then, just before that, you break up with him. Easy as can be."

"Easy for you to say, that is." Nadine looked once more at the offending section, shaking her head. "I still can't believe you did this."

"Hey, I could have put in Clint Fletcher's name."

Nadine shot her a murderous look. "You dare."

"Hey. You could do worse," Donna said with a laugh. "Clint's pretty easy on the eyes and whether you like to admit it or not, I think you agree."

The problem was, she did agree. She agreed most wholeheartedly.

Nadine swatted Donna on the head with the paper and left.

Donna crouched down and filled the cubicle under Sharlene's desk with the latest editions of the paper for walk-in customers. The door jangled and as she straightened, a tall, darkly handsome man stepped through the door. He wore denim jeans and a hunter green cable-knit sweater. He had wavy dark brown hair, and his gray eyes scanned the interior of the office almost hesitantly.

"Can I help you?" Donna asked, curious as to who he was.

He shrugged and slanted her a self-deprecating grin. "I'm actually looking for..." He paused a moment. "Nadine Laidlaw."

"She's in her office right now. Can I ask who wants to see her?"

"Trace Bennet."

Donna felt her jaw drop. "Okay," she said stupidly.

Then she thought, What am I going to tell Nadine? She caught sight of Clint in his office staring at them both, and she knew she had to do something.

"I'll show you to her office." She walked around the high, curved desk, caught Trace Bennet by the arm and literally dragged him down the hallway to Nadine's tiny office. "This is a real surprise. I'm sure Nadine isn't expecting you. She's talked about you, but I've never met you and I'm sure she's never met you..." Donna babbled. "I mean, she would like to meet you." Or maybe not, she thought despairingly. What am I going to do? She'll kill me for sure. She stopped at Nadine's office. Thankfully the door was open.

Nadine looked up from her desk, frowned at Donna and then at Mr. Bennet.

"Nadine," Donna said, her voice falsely cheerful, "such an interesting coincidence." She turned to the good-looking man. "This is, um…"

"What is going on?" Nadine asked, getting up from her desk. Trace stared at Nadine. He looked as if someone had punched him in the stomach.

Looks like it's up to me, thought Donna. "Nadine, I'd like to introduce you to Trace Bennet."

"Oh, dear," Nadine whispered, looking as bewildered as Trace did. "What have I done?"

Trace took a breath and then smiled. "I'm a little confused here."

"*You* are?" Nadine replied. "Please, sit down."

"I think I had better check on some coffee." Donna took a few steps backward, bumping into the door before she beat a hasty retreat.

Nadine sighed and looked once more at Trace Bennet. What coincidence had caused her to come up with this man's name? This man who happened to be very good-looking and frighteningly real, now seated in a chair, smiling hesitantly at her?

"I have to apologize, Mr. Bennet…" She let the sentence drift off. Her usual interviewing skills disappeared.

"That's okay." He smiled and leaned forward. "I'm guessing it was a coincidence. I had to come to this office this morning, anyhow. When I noticed my name and yours in the paper, I thought maybe I should talk to you."

Nadine frowned at him, his name echoing from some other source in her mind. "What did you have to come to the office for?"

"I'm starting a new business and needed to talk to you, as the editor, about covering our opening day. I had sent you some information."

Nadine looked at him, and suddenly it all fell into place. There'd been a letter. A new farm implement dealership. "That's where I got the name."

"Pardon me?" Trace frowned.

"The papers you sent me. I must have pulled your name from there. That night, when Grandma..." She shook her head to clear her thoughts.

"When Grandma..." he prompted.

"It doesn't matter," Nadine replied, feeling embarrassed. "It's a long story and you're a complete stranger who, unfortunately, got caught up in a bunch of lies. I'm very, very sorry."

"No. Don't be. Nothing bad came of it." Trace smiled. "I'm really glad I came down to the office today."

Just then the door opened and Donna bustled in carrying a tray bearing two steaming mugs of coffee and a plate of some broken cookies. "Sorry," she apologized. "I had to rescue the bag from Wally." She almost dropped the tray on the desk by Nadine and was about to execute another hasty exit when Nadine reached over and caught her friend by the arm.

"You've already met Donna, but I bet she didn't tell you that she was instrumental in this whole business." Nadine forced a smile at her friend, squeezing her fingers on her arm.

"What?" Donna sputtered. "You're the one who came up with the name." Donna turned to Trace, pressing one hand against her chest. "Honest. I just worked with the raw material provided to me by my friend Nadine. What I did was just embroidery."

Nadine let go, shaking her head at her friend's duplicity. "I didn't think you'd go and put it in the newspaper for everyone to read...."

"No. I put it in the newspaper for your grandma to read." Donna turned to Nadine, an exasperated expression on her face. "That was the point, wasn't it? To let Grandma know that you had a boyfriend so she would move out of your house and leave you alone?"

"Well, somehow it worked out that the whole county got to read that little tidbit, as well...."

"Excuse me, girls," Trace interrupted with a laugh. "It's really not a problem."

"No?" they both said at once, turning in unison to him.

"No. Not at all. I'm new in town." He lifted his hands in a gesture of surrender. "I wanted to meet Nadine anyway."

"That's great," Donna said, turning to Nadine. "Isn't it, Nadine? Here's your boyfriend. You bring him home to Grandma, tell her that you've found the man of your dreams."

"Just a minute, Donna..." sputtered Nadine, seeing an instant need to take control of the situation. "Mr. Bennet is a complete stranger. He's here to do business." She shook her head, feeling overwhelmed. "I think I've had enough of your helpful schemes."

Trace Bennet clasped his hands behind his head, looking perfectly at ease. "Why don't you tell me the history of this little episode? I think it's the least you can do," he added in a teasing tone.

Nadine bit her lip, looking contritely at him. "If I had known..."

"I said it's okay," he said, grinning. "So I gather there's a grandma in this sordid tale."

Donna sat down beside him, more than ready to fill him in, Nadine could see.

"Donna, maybe you had better see if Sharlene needs any help out front?"

Donna frowned, then, taking the broad hint, stood up. With one more smile at Mr. Bennet.

"Anyhow, the story," Nadine began again. "My grandma has been living with me for the past five years, ever since my mother got sick. I've always been very thankful for what she's done, but she was never content to sit back and let other people live their lives. The problem is she won't rest until her only single granddaughter, being me, is married or, at the least, settled down with a boyfriend."

"Which was supposed to be me," Trace said with a grin.

"Which was *supposed* to be a completely fictional character," Nadine said with emphasis. "Your name popped out one day when I found out she was inviting all kinds of single men over for supper." Nadine lifted her hands in surrender. "I'd had enough and told her that I had a date that night and somehow, I guess from skimming over the material, your name came to mind. Donna ran with it and this is the result."

Trace shook his head, his smile reassuring. "Believe me, I'm not one bit sorry that our names were linked in the newspaper. But now the next question is where do we go from here?"

"We break up, of course." She had to put an end to this for Trace Bennet's sake and her own.

Trace stroked his jaw with one hand, his eyes still on her. "But why? You need a boyfriend and I could use the help of someone who knows the people of this town. I don't think we should end such a compatible match over such a little misunderstanding." He smiled, a dimple winking back at her from beside his mouth.

Nadine felt a softening. Trace had a gentle charm about him, and she was only a weak woman who felt guilty about using this man's name. But the thought of hoodwinking not only her grandma but also the citizens of the town she lived in made her hesitate.

"If we actually went out together, you wouldn't be lying to your grandmother. And dating a beautiful girl like you would hardly be a hardship for me."

Trace stood up, his hands in his pockets. "I don't mind, if you don't."

"No," squeaked Nadine. "Not really."

"Good. We can start off with dinner tonight at the Derwin Inn. You can fill me in on the town and its occupants."

Nadine nodded, feeling once again as if someone was taking control of her life. But as she looked up at Trace's handsome face, she didn't mind.

"Great." He reached out a hand, and automatically Nadine caught it. "It's a deal, then. I'll pick you up from your place tonight and we'll celebrate our first official 'date.'" He winked at her. "Where do you live?"

Nadine gave him her address, then he left and she stared at the closed door, feeling bemused, overwhelmed and oddly satisfied. Trace Bennet was a charming, fine-looking man. And the thought of spending an evening with him made her feel wanted.

Okay, Lord, was this it? Was this the answer to my prayer? She smiled. She figured she would find out in time.

Chapter Five

As Nadine poured herself some tea from a miniature silver pot she looked across the table at Trace, studying him as he stirred his coffee.

He glanced up at her and smiled. "And what is Nadine Laidlaw thinking of now?"

"Actually, I'm wondering why you wanted to take me out." She stopped, realizing how that sounded, then added, "I mean, after what we did to you."

"I'm lonely, I'm new in town and I want to get to know you better." He set his cup down, lowering his voice to a more intimate level. "I've been wondering about you for a while."

Nadine frowned. "What do you mean?"

"I've been subscribing to the paper for a while, reading your articles." He covered her hand with his, twining his fingers through hers. "You are a very principled person. You've got strong values...." He hesitated, squeezing her hand. "That comes out in your writing." He leaned forward, holding her hand tightly now, as if he was afraid to let go. "I want to get to know you better. I think that little mistake your friend made wasn't just a mistake. I think this meeting was meant to be."

Nadine blinked, trying to absorb what he had just said. While his declaration had been pleasant, it created a feeling of discomfort she couldn't put a finger on. Nadine carefully pulled her hand out of his.

He smiled then, easing the intensity of the moment. "I feel it is only right that we spend this evening getting to know each other better." He lifted his coffee cup and took another sip. "Why don't we start with you?"

"I don't know," she said slowly, gathering her thoughts. "There's not much to tell."

"Try me."

Nadine lifted her hands and then, with a laugh, started. "I was born here in Derwin, went to school here, left for about a year to take some journalism classes, came back when my father died and my mother became ill. Got a job at the *Derwin Times,* moved from reporter to editor where I am now."

"That was a concise résumé."

"I've had a concise life." Nadine shrugged. She took a sip of her tea as she looked past him, just in time to see Clint Fletcher get up from the table where he had been sitting. Did he come here all the time?

Clint glanced up and caught her gaze. Disconcerted, she watched as he paused, then sauntered over.

"Hello, Nadine." He turned to Trace, and Nadine had no choice but to introduce them.

"Trace, this is Clint Fletcher, my boss. Fletcher, this is Trace Bennet." She forced a smile. "Trace is starting an implement dealership in town."

Trace stood and held out a hand to Clint. "Pleased to meet you," Trace said. "Would you like to join us?"

But to Nadine's relief Clint shook his head. "No. I have to be on my way." He looked back at Trace, his mouth curved in a polite smile. "Thanks for the offer, though."

"I'll have to make arrangements to talk to you sometime," Trace said, sitting down again. "You can tell me all about Derwin."

Clint glanced at Nadine. "Nadine has spent her entire life here and can probably fill you in better than I can on the goings-on of the town."

Nadine bristled. He made it sound as if she had never been anywhere but Derwin and had no life whatsoever. "Not all of us have rich uncles who can afford to send us off to Europe, Fletcher," she snapped.

"I realize that, Nadine." He held her angry gaze, his own unflinching.

Nadine felt a moment of confusion at the understanding tone of his voice, the sympathy she saw reflected in his hazel eyes. Uncomfortable, she looked away.

Clint jingled the change in his pocket a moment. "I hope you two have a pleasant evening."

"And I hope it is to be the first of many," said Trace, a touch of humor in his voice.

"The first?" Clint asked. Nadine's gaze flew up to his, then she looked away. He paused a moment, then turned and walked away.

She turned to Trace, who was watching her intently. "Your boss has quite a forceful presence, doesn't he?" he remarked.

"When he wants to," she said, her tone abrupt.

"Has he lived here long?"

"No. He moved here when he was in grade twelve and came to live with his uncle, Dory Strepchuk. My old boss. He used to own the paper, and Clint took over from him." Nadine took a sip of her tea, now cool, and set it down with a grimace. She didn't want to talk about her boss. She could still feel his eyes on her, assessing Trace. For some reason she didn't want him to see her and Trace together.

"But you seem to know him well."

"I should." Nadine laughed shortly. "He went out with my older sister and flirted with the younger one."

"You have sisters?"

Nadine spun her teacup. "Two. Sabrina and Leslie. Both tall, blond, gorgeous."

"Why do you put yourself down like that?" he asked.

Nadine shrugged, uncomfortable with his scrutiny. "It's not a put-down. Merely the facts."

"Well, it sounded as if you were putting yourself down, as well." He sounded displeased. "You're a very attractive person." His gaze was intent. "You have such beautiful deep brown eyes, and such lovely hair." He paused as he looked her face over.

Nadine tried not to feel uncomfortable, tried not to let herself believe what he was telling her.

He sighed a moment. "You have an earthy beauty...."

"Wholesome." Nadine couldn't keep the dour note out of her voice as she said that, nor was she able to stop the faint flush that crept up her cheeks at his kind words. "You can stop now."

"I will. For now." He winked at her. "So now I know that you have two sisters and a grandma. How about your parents?" he prompted.

Nadine looked down at her tea, curving her fingers around the cup as if trying to warm it up. "My father was killed in a logging accident about six years ago. My mother died about six months ago."

"I'm so sorry to hear that."

Nadine lifted one shoulder negligently. "She had ALS, Lou Gehrig's disease. It was better." She looked up at him, anxious to change the subject. Her mother's death wasn't news, but lately it seemed to bring up sorrow and regrets that she didn't want to deal with, not in front of a stranger, no matter how kind he might be.

Thankfully the waitress came with their food. Nadine automatically bent her head in prayer.

When she looked up, he was looking at her with a bemused expression. "I think that's wonderful. Seeing someone who isn't afraid to show what they believe."

Nadine didn't know what to say. Her belief was not something to take credit or be praised for.

"I'm glad that you aren't afraid to pray in public," he continued. He tilted his head as he looked at her, his gaze intent. "You are a very special person, Nadine. Your faith comes through in your writing, as well."

Nadine couldn't think of anything to say. His words spoke to her own longing for a soul mate, someone she could share her faith with. "I've been blessed with a believing family," she said quietly. "I know I want the same for myself."

"Not everyone gets that," he said, his voice tinged with pain. Then with a shake of his head he dispelled the mood. "And you have been blessed."

"And what about your family?"

And Trace told her about the Bennets. They still lived in the Fraser Valley and had a dairy farm. Trace had worked for a local implement dealer and from there had moved up. Now he was poised to start his own business. He had been scouting likely locations for the past year and had settled on Derwin.

"But I've been looking for more than just a place to build a dealership." He winked at Nadine. "I sure didn't expect to find such a good-looking date this quickly."

Nadine tried not to blush at how that had come about. It was still very embarrassing. "Let's not talk about that one, okay?" she pleaded.

"How many times do I have to tell you? I'm really enjoying myself." He shook his head. "Now you have to tell me more about yourself. What about your hopes, your dreams?"

Hopes and dreams? Had she even had an opportunity in the past years to articulate what she wanted, to figure it out?

"Stuck?" he prodded.

She shook her head. "It seems that I've spent so much time taking care of my mother and working that I don't know if I've even had a chance lately to hope and dream." She looked back at Trace and dismissed her melancholy with a light laugh. "I guess I have to believe that God put me here for a reason and I'll find out what that is in His time."

"God's ways are mysterious, that's for sure." Trace smiled as they shared a moment of accord.

The rest of the evening went by far too quickly and soon it was time to go. As he pulled up to her building, Nadine noticed one light burning in the living room of her apartment. Grandma was waiting up.

They walked into the building and Trace stopped at the door to her apartment, spinning out their farewell.

"Will I be able to see you soon, next time I'm in

town?" Trace picked up her hand, playing with her fingers.

"Sure," Nadine said, suppressing a trill of anticipation. "Thanks for a lovely evening. I enjoyed it thoroughly."

The door creaked behind them as it opened slowly. "Nadine, are you still out there?"

Nadine stiffened at the sound of her grandmother's voice. "Yes, Grandma."

"Well, come in, right now." Grandma pushed the door open and stepped out into the hallway, wrapping her fleece robe tightly around her. "It's late."

Nadine glanced back at Trace, who, thankfully, hadn't changed expression at the sight of this diminutive woman.

"Trace, this is my Grandma Laidlaw. Grandma, this is Trace Bennet."

Grandma kept her hands around her waist and only nodded in acknowledgment. "So I finally get to meet you, Mr. Bennet."

"Pleased to meet you." Trace held out his hand to Grandma. She took it begrudgingly and quickly shook it. "And please call me Trace."

"I will." She looked him over once and then turned away as if he wasn't worth any more of her time. "I want you to come in, Nadine. It's late and I'm sure both you and Mr. Bennet have an early day at work tomorrow."

"I'll be in shortly, Grandma," Nadine replied in a warning tone.

Danielle was unrepentant. She glanced once more

in Trace's general direction. "Nice to meet you," she said abruptly, her tone conveying anything but. As she left, Nadine turned apologetically to Trace.

"Sorry about her. She takes notions. And the notion she has in her grip tonight is that she refuses to like anyone she hasn't picked for me herself."

"That's okay." Trace slid his hands into his pockets, hunching his shoulders. "But I still want to see you again." He winked at her and straightened. For a moment Nadine thought he was going to kiss her, but he only touched her cheek with one finger. "I'll call," he said softly. Then, turning, he left.

Nadine watched him go, a sigh lifting her shoulders. She walked to the glass doors and watched as he drove away.

After she'd dropped Jack and come back to Derwin, she hadn't had time to date. Since her mother's illness she hadn't gone on a real date until tonight.

Nadine wrinkled her nose and laughed shortly. And even that date had been manufactured.

"Special delivery for you, Nadine." Sharlene breezed into Nadine's office two days later carrying a huge bouquet of white roses.

Nadine reached for the flowers, surprised, pleased. Flowers. "Who are they from?"

"That's what I'd like to know. Here, this came with." Sharlene handed Nadine an envelope. Nadine opened it and pulled out the small card, then smiled. Trace.

She went off in search of a vase, carrying the flowers with her. She found a jar and was returning to her office, her nose buried in the bouquet, when she literally bumped into Clint Fletcher.

He caught her by the elbows and steadied her, his eyes on the flowers.

"A secret admirer?" he said, his expression serious.

"This one's not a secret," she said with a smile. "They came from Trace."

He cocked an eyebrow at her, still not smiling. "The boyfriend?"

Nadine didn't like the ironic tone of his voice. "Yes. They were delivered here this morning," she answered.

"Well. He's certainly expressing his affection in an atypical fashion." Clint flicked a finger at the flowers. "I always labored under the impression that red roses were the flower of choice in a romance."

Where does he haul out that language? thought Nadine. "Well, labor no more, Fletcher. These days anything goes." Nadine took a noisy sniff of her flowers, her eyes on Clint.

"It would seem that way," Clint said dryly.

"Clint, can you come here a moment?" Wally, the other reporter, called out from the end of the hallway.

She turned and watched him go, puzzled at his comment and his attitude.

Shrugging off Clint's reaction, she returned to her

office. She had a few calls to make, some follow-up work to do and had to go over her mail.

And it was Clint's and her turn to "Face Off."

The weekly column was Dory Strepchuk's legacy. Each week two of the staff of any of the three sister papers would take an opposing view on a controversial topic. This week, by some twist of fate, she and Clint had to go head-to-head on the topic "Should the Government Bail Out Large Companies?" Thankfully Clint had chosen the "yes" side.

And that would be okay with her.

Her phone was ringing as she stepped into her office. It was Trace.

"Get my flowers?" he asked.

"I did. Thanks so much. They're beautiful."

"Not as beautiful as you are." Trace chuckled. "I know that's a pretty corny line, but it's true. And you're simply supposed to say thank-you."

Nadine tried not to take his compliment seriously. "Thanks, Trace. They are very lovely."

"Got them just because. I miss you, you know."

"Now I know you're laying it on thick. We only met two days ago."

"I don't feel like that, Nadine," he said, his tone suddenly serious. "I feel like we've met years ago...like I've been waiting for someone like you...."

For once, Nadine didn't know what to say. Trace almost seemed too good to be true.

"I'm coming back to town on Thursday. I know there's a new movie showing in Eastbar. I thought we could go out for supper and then hit the movie. Just like we did last week.'' He laughed. ''Is that okay with you?''

Nadine couldn't help the smile that curved her lips. ''Sounds wonderful.''

''I'm looking forward to it, Nadine.'' He was quiet a moment. ''I know this sounds silly, but I really feel like we're meant for each other, Nadine. I'm looking forward to getting to know you better.''

''Me, too,'' was all she could say. ''Me, too.''

'''Why do we allow our government to bail out megacorporations who have not shown themselves to be responsible corporate citizens,''' read Nadine out loud, '''and ignore the daily bankruptcy of any number of small, home-based businesses, owned by families and in financial difficulty because of circumstances beyond their control? Many large corporations are not even North American owned, but are subsidiaries of companies whose ownership is lost in a morass of paper shuffling and numbered companies. Is their plight more important than that of native North Americans?''' Nadine folded the papers with a grin and set them on the table at the Downtown Deli. ''And my column goes on to make many more very scintillating points.''

''Very well done,'' agreed Donna, pulling a sprout out of her bagel. ''Emotional, but well done.''

''Of course it's emotional. It's an editorial.''

''Well, you tend to be more shrill whenever you

write about anything even remotely connected to Skyline."

"No, I'm not."

Donna shrugged away the objection. "Anyway, it's good."

Nadine smiled. Encouraging words to a writer were food and drink. "Thanks. I think it's going to be a great match for the Skyline article I pulled out of the computer."

Donna examined her bagel more closely, her expression suddenly serious. "You still going to run that?"

"Probably."

"I thought Clint asked you to back off."

"He did. But I'm not going to. This is too important."

"Why are you deliberately antagonizing the poor guy? Clint's going to end up in trouble over it."

"I had an empty spot I needed to fill," Nadine said defensively. "With the column it's a perfect fit. Skyline has been on the receiving end of a few kickbacks and government grants." Nadine winked at Donna, trying to alleviate her serious mood. "Besides, no one had anything else besides photos of beaming farmers holding up monster vegetables."

"Why don't you leave poor Clint alone?" Donna continued. "He's got enough on his plate."

"What do you mean by that?"

Donna took the last bite of her bagel, frowning. "A nagging partner, a potential lawsuit and a stubborn employee who won't listen. That's more than enough," she mumbled. She finished her bagel and wiped her fingers off with a napkin. "But you don't want to talk about Clint, so tell me about your date with Trace instead."

Nadine knew she was touchy on the subject of Clint Fletcher and gladly took up the change in topic. "He's very nice. He's funny. He's good-looking."

"And Grandma?"

Nadine blew out her breath. "She's coming around." Which was stretching the truth about 175 degrees.

"So now that she's met your boyfriend, is she going to give up? Move out?"

Nadine picked up her sandwich, avoiding Donna's questioning look. "She hasn't said."

"I gather he doesn't meet with her full approval."

Nadine shook her head and took a bite of her sandwich.

"So what are you going to do?"

"I don't know." Nadine studied her sandwich.

"I don't know why you have so much trouble with her." Donna leaned forward, smiling. "Goodness knows, she's smaller than you."

"She's also incredibly stubborn and obtuse. And when I try to get really definite, she gently reminds me of all she did for me and my mom." Nadine picked at her bread. "That's where I usually cave."

"That's easy enough. Take some of the stuff you dish out to Clint and save it for Grandma. Might work."

"What is with you?" Nadine asked, surprised at the return to her boss. "I don't know what comments you're talking about."

"Those snide comments you're always tossing at him. You could use them on Grandma."

"I wouldn't do that. I love my grandma."

"And you dislike Clint?" Donna shook her head as she wiped her mouth.

"I don't dislike him. We just seem to strike sparks off each other." Sparks that made her remarkably uneasy.

"I think you do more striking than he does."

"Where does that come from?" asked Nadine, uncomfortable with what her friend inferred. "How come all of a sudden you're on his side?"

Donna sat back and dug in her purse for some change. "I'm not on anyone's 'side.' I've just been watching you and him, and if I didn't know any better—" she got up and dropped a dollar coin on the table "—I'd say you had a crush on the man."

"Are you crazy?" Nadine scrambled to her feet, dragging her camera bag along with her. "Where in the world do you come off saying something like that?"

Donna glanced at her irate friend as she waited for change from the cashier. "If you don't like him, why do you pay so much attention to him?" She held out her hand for the change. "Thanks, Iris. And you have yourself a good day."

Donna sauntered out of the Deli, leaving behind a confused Nadine and an obviously interested Iris.

Nadine paid the cashier as well, then caught up to her friend.

"Okay. What were you talking about back there?" Nadine jogged up beside Donna.

Donna stopped. "I was talking about the way you treat Clint. You can't seem to resist any chance to give him a dig or some kind of snide comment."

Nadine frowned, trying to think why Donna would say that. "I don't treat him that bad." She thought back to comments she had made to Clint, trying to see them from Donna's viewpoint. "I mean, I needle him, but that's just for fun."

"You may think so. But it doesn't come out that way."

"Well, he's just as bad."

Donna crossed her arms and looked her friend directly in the eye. "How?" she asked quietly.

Nadine looked away, rubbing her hand along the strap of her bag, trying to remember. "Give me a couple of days. I'll come up with something."

Donna nodded knowingly. "The truth is you can't come up with any one incident. And if you can't think of any time he's been miserable to you, maybe you might want to spend that time wondering why you pay so much attention to him." She winked at Nadine and stepped into the office.

Nadine leaned against the window. Clint was always ragging on her, always trying to find a way to make her flustered.

Wasn't he...?

Nadine bit her lip, convinced she could find *something*.

But after a few minutes she came to a disarming realization.

Clint had never talked to her the way she talked to him. And Donna was right. It was no way for a Christian to treat another person.

Chapter Six

"You're wearing a skirt to work, Nadine?" Grandma set her cup of tea down and stared at her granddaughter as she stepped into the kitchen.

"Trace is picking me up right after work for a date tonight."

She had topped the skirt with a loose sweater and, in a fit of whimsy, wound a gauzy patterned scarf around her neck, tucking the ends in. She had curled her hair and taken time to brush her eyelashes with mascara and her eyelids with a faint dusting of gold eye shadow. She couldn't recall when she'd purchased the rarely worn makeup—maybe for Leslie's wedding? Or was it Sabrina's? Nadine was surprised that the old mascara hadn't dried up.

"You look very nice," Grandma said approvingly. "The makeup looks good, as well. Sets off your pretty eyes."

"Thanks, Grandma." Nadine laughed as she bent

over and kissed Danielle's cheek. "It's been so long since I wore makeup, I'm trying not to feel like a store mannequin," she admitted, sitting down to her breakfast. She also wondered if she was going to make it to the end of the day before the hair hanging around her jawline drove her nuts.

"Well, you're going to turn a few heads, I'm sure." Grandma smiled her approval and Nadine felt a little better. "Clint Fletcher won't recognize you."

"I didn't do this for my boss," Nadine said more sharply than she had intended.

"Of course not." Danielle smiled. "I'm sure Trace will like the way you look."

Nadine was somewhat mollified by her grand-mother's encouraging comments. "Thanks, Grandma."

They ate their breakfast in silence, Grandma read-ing the paper and Nadine going over her notes for the interview she was going to do tomorrow. When Nadine left the apartment she felt ready to face the world.

"Good morning, Sharlene." Nadine breezed into the office, pausing at the mail drop to check for any mail or messages.

Sharlene looked up from an ad she was writing out with a smile that froze on her face when she caught sight of her editor. "Nadine?" she said, her voice weak with surprise.

Nadine grinned back and flipped a hand through her hair. "Do I look *that* different today?"

"Different enough." Sharlene shook her head.

"The Nadine I know wouldn't wear a skirt except to church, and she certainly would never put on makeup."

Nadine smiled as she looked down at the envelopes in her hands. "People change," she murmured.

"Do they ever." Clint's disbelieving voice behind her made her head snap up.

Nadine kept her eyes straight ahead, feeling suddenly self-conscious about her clothes, her makeup, her hair.

What does it matter what he thinks? she reminded herself. He's just your boss. She curved her lips into a smile and turned to face Clint, who stood in the doorway of his office, one shoulder propped against the doorjamb, his eyebrows raised in surprise.

A sharp retort to deflect his comment came to mind, but on its heels, Donna's admonition from the day before. She hesitated, catching his eye. Clint's expression became serious as the moment stretched out. He straightened, his eyelids lowering slightly, his lips softening. She couldn't look away and, for some puzzling reason, didn't want to.

Flustered, she shuffled through the envelopes, dropping a couple. As she bent to pick them up, other hands beat her to it. Without looking up at Clint, she took them from him and escaped to her office.

What is wrong with you? she chided herself as she dropped her knapsack on the floor beside her desk. She shook her head as if to rearrange her thoughts and dropped the mail onto her already overflowing desk. Clint Fletcher is your boss, you are Nadine Laidlaw and you dressed up for your date with Trace.

She walked around her desk to turn on her computer. She had set today aside to clear off some paperwork and do some more work on some of the columns she had written. With a little luck she would be finished by the time Trace came tonight to pick her up.

She looked over her articles, skipped lunch and headed out to do an interview.

Trace phoned while Nadine was away, and left the message that he would pick her up from the office a little later than he had originally planned. Nadine didn't mind. It gave her a little more time to finish off some stories.

She spent the better part of the afternoon looking over the résumés of people who had applied for the other reporter's job. She desperately needed someone to help out. She and Wally were each doing a job and a half to make up for the vacancy, and it was wearing both of them down. Clint helped out where he could, but the workload was still too much.

The day seemed to fly by. When Nadine finally pushed herself back from her computer, she was surprised to see it was almost five-forty.

Blinking tiredly, she lifted a hand to rub her eyes. Just in time she remembered her mascara and stopped herself.

Nadine clicked her mouse to save the file she was

working on and then shut down her computer. She
didn't want to work anymore. Trace would be coming for her any moment.

She rolled her neck, looking with satisfaction over
her desk, pleased with the empty spaces she could
now see. She had another interview to do tomorrow
and Saturday a volleyball tournament to cover.
Thankfully this one was in town, so she wouldn't
have to travel. Trace wanted to take her out Saturday, as well.

She went to the bathroom and checked her
makeup, brushed her hair and tried to still the butterflies in her stomach.

A date. After all these years, she was going on a
date. She grinned at herself in the mirror. And not
a date of Grandma's doing. A date with someone
who wanted to be with her. Nadine tilted her head
as she studied her reflection. She wasn't a vain person, but the fact that someone wanted to be with her
made her take a second look at the young woman
in the mirror. She winked at her reflection and
walked out.

Half an hour later, Trace still hadn't come. Nadine
had busied herself with odd jobs, cleaning out the
coffee room, gathering a few mugs from different
places in the office, trying to quell her nervous tension. What if he wasn't coming?

She tried not to, but periodically she walked down
the hall to the front door to see if Trace was waiting
outside. He wasn't, and Nadine wondered how long
she should wait.

She made a fresh pot of coffee and leaned against the counter, waiting for the machine to finish dripping, an unwelcome feeling of melancholy coming over her. She decided she would give Trace another fifteen minutes and then she would…

She would what? she thought, her stomach tightening at the thought of facing her grandmother, telling her that she had been stood up.

The soft hiss of the coffee machine broke the stillness of the room. Nadine used to dread this time of the day. For the past year any free evenings she had were spent at the hospital. The last few months of her mother's life were fraught with tension and wondering. Each time the phone rang, Nadine and her grandmother wondered if this time it was the hospital. Her sisters came whenever they could, but Nadine knew they didn't have the time she had. That meant the bulk of the visiting and doctor's consultations fell on Nadine's shoulders.

The memories always brought tears, and tonight was no exception. Nadine felt the nudge of pain and closed her eyes as it drifted over her. She tried to fight it, but couldn't.

I miss her, Lord, she prayed, pressing her hand against her mouth, tears sliding down her cheeks as the pain increased. *I know she's better off where she is, but I still miss her so much.* She drew in a deep breath, wishing she could stop the tears.

A noise behind her broke abruptly into her sorrow. She whirled around, her heart pounding.

"Sorry." Clint stood in the doorway of the coffee

room, his tie loosened, his cuffs rolled up. "I didn't know you were still here."

Nadine turned away again, surreptitiously wiping at her cheeks. "That's fine," she replied, looking around for a napkin, anything to get rid of the mortifying tears.

"Nadine." He came toward her, his deep voice tinged with concern. "Is something wrong?"

She snatched up some napkins and hurriedly wiped at her eyes. "Do you want some coffee?" she asked, her voice muffled by the napkin.

"I can get it," he replied, stepping past her, thankfully not glancing her way. He stood with his broad back to her, his shirt pulling across his shoulders as he reached up for a cup. He poured himself some coffee and then glanced over his shoulder at her.

"I'm sorry if I embarrassed you." He turned to face her. "I don't mean to intrude."

Nadine looked down at the crumpled napkin, now smeared with mascara. She shook her head at her own clumsiness. "I'm fine" was all she could manage.

"Has something happened?" he persisted.

Nadine hesitated, her previous encounters with Clint creating a barrier. She remembered once again Donna's admonition. He had been a visitor in their home any number of times, had met her mother and knew Grandma. He had been a large part of her life for a time. He was kind of an old friend, she had to concede. He could be told the truth.

"Nothing happened," Nadine said with a shaky smile. She took a deep breath to steady her voice. "I just...miss my mother." She bit back another soft cry and could speak no more. Another set of tears drifted down her cheeks.

Clint said nothing, and for that Nadine was thankful. He stood, quiet, waiting, listening. His gaze serious, interested. Sympathetic with no trace of pity.

Nadine took another deep breath, studying the smeared napkin. "Silly, isn't it? She's been dead six months and it seems like I'm sadder now than I was when she died."

"Six months isn't that long," he replied softly. "I would think it takes years to get over the death of someone you love."

Nadine nodded. "I remember my mom crying over my dad even just until a couple of years ago."

"I don't know if you ever get over the death of someone you care for. I think it's quite something that your mother loved your father like that." Clint laughed shortly. "You were lucky to see that while you were growing up."

Nadine paused, looking at him, surprised at this admission. "You were never close to your parents, were you?" she asked.

Clint shook his head, smiling sadly. "Hard to be close to a couple who seldom talked to each other, let alone their son." He looked up at Nadine, his gaze sincere. "I used to hate them, but I realized that it only drained whatever joy I could find in my life. I'm thankful that I found a loving Father who cares for me with a strength and sincerity I haven't found on earth. I learned that and much more from Uncle Dory and am thankful for more reasons than one that I was sent here to Derwin.''

Nadine was taken aback at his admission. Clint had never been very forthcoming about his spiritual life.

''I always admired your mother's strength,'' Clint continued, setting down his coffee cup. ''She did a good job raising you girls, teaching you the right things, encouraging you in your relationship with God. I'm sure she must have been proud of you.''

Nadine shrugged. ''Well, at least Sabrina and Leslie managed to get themselves married.''

Clint said nothing to that and Nadine sniffed once again, wiping at her eyes.

''You have nothing to be ashamed of,'' Clint said finally. ''Jack was a fool to let you go.''

Nadine looked up at that, blinking away more tears as she caught Clint's steady gaze. She looked at him again, as if seeing him with new eyes.

A sudden knocking on the front door startled them both. ''Hello, anybody there?'' Trace's muffled voice drifted down the hallway.

''Well. Looks like your date is finally here,'' said Clint, his voice dry.

Nadine turned to leave, but was surprised when Clint caught her arm to stop her. ''Just a minute,'' he said, picking up a napkin. He tugged on her arm to bring her closer. ''Your mascara is smudged,'' he said.

Nadine felt a most curious sensation as she looked up. His hazel eyes seemed to draw her in, pull her toward him. She felt the warmth of his hand encircling her arm, his fingers brushing her cheek as he wiped a smudge away. She raised her hand to rest it on his shoulder as she felt herself drift toward him.

Another loud knock on the door broke the moment.

"You better go before your ardent suitor breaks down the door," said Clint dryly, letting her go.

Nadine nodded, feeling suddenly breathless. She stopped at the doorway, looking back. But Clint had his coffee in his hand and was sipping it, his eyes downcast.

Shaking off the feelings he had aroused in her, she turned and ran down the hallway.

"Wow. Do you ever look terrific," Trace greeted her appreciatively. "I didn't think you could get even more gorgeous."

Nadine smiled, passing off his compliments with a dismissive gesture.

Trace caught her hands. "I know exactly what that means, you silly girl. Hey, sorry I'm late," he said. "I got stuck at the bank." He pulled her closer and kissed her lightly on her cheek. "Forgive me?"

"I was wondering if you were going to stand me up."

"Are you kidding?" Trace pulled her close to him. "A guy would have to be crazy to do that to someone like you." He kissed her again. "The movie just started. We can grab supper later."

Nadine ran back down the hallway and got her purse from her office. She stepped out the door and, pausing a moment, walked back to the coffee room. Clint still stood at the counter, his coffee cup in his hands.

He looked at her. "Still here?" was all he said.

Nadine bit her lip, unable to pass off what had just happened, unsure of what to make of it. "Thanks," she said finally, hoping he understood what she meant. "For everything."

Clint nodded. "Any time, Nadine," he replied softly. "Any time at all."

"C'mon, gorgeous," Trace called. "The night isn't getting any younger."

"See you Monday," she said, then turned and left.

Nadine cranked on the film rewind as the noise of the celebrating team roiled around her. It was Saturday night. The home team had won their invitational volleyball tournament and were celebrating in the true manner of high school champions.

They were screaming their fool heads off.

Nadine popped open her camera, pulled the film out and, crouching down, dropped it into an empty canister and popped the top on. She was finished for the night.

"There you are." Trace's voice behind her made her whirl around in surprise. He wore a denim jacket tonight, blue jeans and cowboy boots. He looked like a rodeo poster boy, rugged and almost too handsome.

"Hi." She smiled up at him and he reached out and tucked a strand of hair behind her ear. "You're early."

"I'm even earlier than you think. I watched the final game."

"They're pretty good, aren't they?"

"I wouldn't know." He took her bag from her and pulled her close. "I kept getting distracted by this cute reporter on the sidelines snapping pictures."

Nadine just shook her head at his lavish compliments. As they passed a group of celebrating teenagers, a few of the girls cast admiring glances Trace's way. Nadine knew she shouldn't feel proud, but she did. Nothing boosted a girl's ego more than knowing that other women, no matter how young, thought your escort was good-looking.

She looked up at him and caught him smiling down at her. He dropped a quick kiss on her forehead and drew her closer. "I missed you, Nadine," he said.

Nadine looked away, her feelings uncertain. On the one hand she felt inundated with his charm, his obvious attraction to her, yet she couldn't help but feel uncomfortable with how quickly he'd seemed to lay a claim to her. This was only the second time they had been together, not counting their first "date." His intensity didn't seem right, for a reason she couldn't put her finger on.

They walked out to his truck and as they did, Nadine's cell phone rang. She pulled it out and answered it. It was Grandma.

"I'll be home in a while, Grandma. Don't wait up for me." Nadine rolled her eyes at Danielle's response, then ended the phone call.

"Handy things, aren't they?" Trace said with a grin as he unlocked the door for her.

"Not really. I wish I didn't have to carry it around, even though it is a great tool for a reporter." Nadine got into the car and laid the phone on the seat as she buckled up.

"Where do you want to go tonight?" Trace asked as he started up the car and reversed out of the school parking lot.

Nadine shrugged, stifling a yawn. She had been busy all day and hadn't given a thought to dinner.

"You look tired," Trace said as he pulled into the street. "How about someplace quiet?" He grinned at her and, gunning the engine, headed down the street.

Nadine felt a little better once she'd eaten supper. Trace was stimulating company and he made her laugh. The talk stayed light, something for which Nadine was grateful. She was tired and was also thankful when Trace said that he had to leave early.

"Looks like your grandma is still up," he commented as they walked up to the apartment.

"She likes to stay up until I'm home. Says you never know what might happen." Nadine shook her head. "I'd invite you in, but with Grandma still up..."

Trace shrugged. "I don't want to bother her. Besides, I'll be coming here tomorrow after church. If that's okay," he added quickly.

Nadine smiled back, a feeling of well-being bubbling up in her. "I'm looking forward to it."

Trace caught her close, and just as he was about to lower his head to kiss her, a cough sounded in the hallway behind them.

"Nadine, are you coming in?" Danielle demanded, her gray head poking out into the hallway, her voice querulous.

Trace pulled back and winked at Nadine. "I should let you go." He ran a finger lightly down her chin and then looked past her. "Hello, Mrs. Laidlaw. How are you?"

"Tired," said Grandma succinctly.

"I'm sorry." He looked back at Nadine. "I guess this is good-night?"

Nadine nodded, curiously glad Grandma had shown up. She felt once again that Trace was moving too quickly. Too quickly for her, anyway.

Trace ran a finger gently down her cheek. "I'll see you at church tomorrow?"

"I'd like that," she said softly.

"Good." He winked at her and then, with a quick wave at Grandma, turned and left.

Nadine watched as he pulled open the doors and sauntered down the walk. He got in the truck, waved at Nadine and drove away.

"So," Grandma said from behind her. "Why didn't he come in?"

Nadine sighed and turned to face her grandma. "Because I think he's a little afraid of you."

Danielle "humphed" at that. "He looks a little too polished for my liking."

"How can you say that? He wears blue jeans and cowboy boots."

Danielle just shrugged and sat down on a kitchen chair. "It's just an impression."

Nadine turned on the tap and filled a glass with cold water. "I don't know why you don't like him."

"I don't dislike him, Naddy. What a thing to say." Danielle sounded hurt.

Nadine gulped down the water and set the glass on the sink. "You don't treat him very well. The last time he stopped by here, he asked me what I had told you about him."

Danielle fingered the belt of her housecoat, her eyes downcast. "I don't trust him, Naddy," she said softly, her voice suddenly quiet. She looked up, her blue eyes softened with concern. "I'm just not comfortable with him. I would much prefer it if you were to go out with…"

Nadine held a hand up. "Stop right there, Grandma." She tilted her head sideways, studying her grandmother as realization dawned. "I think you don't like him because you didn't handpick him for me yourself."

"I already said I don't dislike him," protested Danielle.

"Well, then, treat him better tomorrow, because he's coming over," Nadine announced, a warning note in her voice.

"I will, Nadine. I'm not rude."

"No, you're not," conceded Nadine. "But I know how you can smile and sting at the same time."

"I'll be very kind and considerate."

But Danielle didn't have to exert herself to that extent, because Trace didn't show up at church the next day and consequently didn't come to the Laidlaw residence for the Sunday lunch Nadine had risen so early to prepare.

Nadine tried to hide her disappointment and Danielle tried to hide her triumph. Neither were very successful. As a result, Sunday was not the blessing it should have been.

Chapter Seven

Nadine spread the latest edition of the *Derwin Times* out, propped her elbows on the desk and began her Tuesday-morning, once-weekly hunt for typos. It didn't matter how up-to-date the technology or how eagle-eyed their copy editor, on a good day only one typo slipped through, on a bad...

Nadine sighed, pulled out her red pen and circled the spelling mistake that jumped off the page at her.

She glanced over a few more articles, turned a few more pages, then stopped at her article on Skyline. She skimmed over it, then reread it to make sure she had been balanced and fair.

Nadine frowned, trying to read it critically, always difficult when the words were so familiar. It had taken her a couple of drafts to get it just right.

"Their labor practices are questionable, and when they were asked for a copy of their safety code, this reporter was brushed off. What do they have to hide? And why do they continue to obtain government grants by fair means or foul..." Nadine read. And it got stronger after that.

Because when it came to Skyline, she had emotion to spare. Nadine sat back and closed her eyes, reliving once again the helpless anger and frustration and grief of her father's life wasted by a company that lied. So much had been taken away from them, with so little explanation.

I want to bring these guys to justice, Lord, she prayed, as she so often did when she thought of Skyline and all the sorrow their actions had caused. *Show me the right way, show me how to do this.* But the prayer brought no peace, no answer. She knew only that she felt better doing *something* instead of merely sitting back, a helpless David facing down an indifferent Goliath.

"Call for you on line one, Nadine. Oh, and some woman phoned a few minutes ago. Didn't leave her name."

Drawing in a deep breath, Nadine picked up the phone. "Nadine Laidlaw here."

Trace greeted her cheerfully. In an hour he was going to be meeting her at the restaurant, and from there he would accompany her to the school meeting she had offered to cover. Nadine would be the happiest when they found a new reporter. Covering for a missing reporter kept her and Wally busier than she liked.

"How are you?" she asked.

"I had to run into Edmonton to meet with one of

the company execs that I'll be working with. I won't be back on time, so keep your cell phone handy.''

Nadine hated taking her phone into meetings. It was disrupting, and it annoyed her to be at her phone's mercy. ''So what time will you be back?''

''I have a better idea. I'll meet you at the inn after your meeting, say, nine-thirty?''

Nadine sighed her disappointment. ''Okay,'' she said softly.

''Hey, sweetie, I'm sorry.''

''Of course you are.'' She tried not to remember Sunday and his broken promise then, as well. It shouldn't matter as much as it did. She still wasn't sure how she felt about Trace, but it was so wonderful to be wanted, to look forward to being with someone. ''I'll see you later, then.'' At least coffee with him was better than nothing.

She hung up the phone and fell back against her chair. Not an auspicious start to the week, she thought.

An abrupt rap on the door made her sit up. ''Come in,'' she called, folding up the newspaper.

It was Clint.

He dropped the newspaper on her desk and stood in front of her, his eyes narrowed.

''I thought you weren't going to run the article,'' he said tightly.

Nadine looked at the paper, folded open to her story on Skyline. ''That was your idea, Fletcher, not mine.''

''I called you into my office last week and asked

you not to run the story.'' His voice was even, but Nadine could hear the suppressed anger.

Nadine steeled herself to look up into Clint's irate eyes so close to hers, trying not to remember their time in the coffee room. ''The article is correct, and the facts have been verified by enough people that I feel more than justified in running it,'' she replied, her own anger building. ''I also told you that we could call an editor's meeting and make a diplomatic decision on whether to run it or not.''

Clint looked down at her, his hand resting on her desk. ''It shouldn't have to come to a showdown of authority, Nadine.''

''Maybe not,'' she acknowledged, ''but an editor of a paper should be just that. An editor. Last I checked, that gives me certain authority and say in what goes into the paper.''

''And last I checked, my name is on the masthead, as well.'' He straightened. ''As the owner.'' He looked down at her, holding her challenging gaze. ''I wish we could work together on this, Nadine,'' he said with a sigh.

Nadine watched him, her heart doing a slow flip. He suddenly looked vulnerable. And for a brief moment she felt a stirring of pity, mingled with attraction. It bothered her more than she cared to admit. It hearkened back to numerous daydreams she had spun over him years ago—and if she dared to admit it, even more recently.

And now, to her dismay, it seemed as if all those dreams and emotions were threatening to undermine her. Taking a deep breath, she concentrated on Skyline and the pain they had caused her family. "I don't know if we can," she said, her voice more sharp than she intended. "Skyline has blood on their hands. Men have died working for them. We have a responsibility to stop them."

"Your father among the lives lost," he said quietly.

Nadine nodded.

Clint blew out his breath and rubbed his neck. "And this is going to help?" he asked, indicating the open newspaper.

Nadine stood up and drew in a steadying breath. "I intend to serve notice to them that we report on more than just local sports and library board meetings." She leaned forward as if to emphasize her point. "We have a God-given duty to expose companies like Skyline. They're crooks and liars, and if they did the same thing in Calgary or Edmonton, they'd have a pack of reporters on their back." She drew in a breath, afraid she was beginning to sound shrill. "I really need to do this, Clint."

Clint looked across the desk at her, his features softening. "I understand why..."

Nadine waited for him to say more, but he didn't. Their gazes met, locked, and it seemed that all else, for that moment, drifted away. Nadine felt gripped by the same curious feeling she had felt the other evening in the coffee room. Once again she felt the tug of attraction, the pull of his personality, and she knew that the feelings that were surfacing were the same ones that had plagued her so long ago.

She forced herself to look down, to break the intense connection with his eyes, busying herself with the newspapers on the desk.

She refolded his newspaper and handed it back to him, her eyes going no farther than his dark tie cinched around the collar of his gray shirt. "Here's your paper," she said.

Clint cleared his throat. "Thanks," he said as he took it. He tapped the paper against his thigh, still towering over her.

He hesitated, then finally left.

When the door closed behind him, Nadine pressed her fingers to her eyes as once again she felt a rush of tears. She dropped her face into her hands, and in the privacy of her office allowed the confusion of her emotions to overwhelm her.

She missed her father, she still grieved her mother. She felt alone, though surrounded by people who cared for her. She had been put off by Trace for the second time in two days.

And now she was falling for Clint Fletcher all over again.

How do these things happen, she wondered. How can a heart work so totally independent of a mind?

Was she an idiot? How could she fall for a man whose presence intimidated her so much that she resorted to deflecting his attention with cutting comments?

She looked heavenward. *Why, Lord? Why am I*

*falling for this man? He doesn't like me that way,
never has. Please take away these feelings. Please.*

She stopped, as if waiting for something, anything. A feeling of reassurance, a still, small voice
guiding her, helping her. But she felt nothing, heard
nothing. Nadine felt as if her prayers went only as
far as the ceiling above her.

And later that evening, as she sat alone in the inn,
waiting in vain for Trace, she wondered what she
had done to deserve the loneliness that seemed to
surround her.

"Two cameras, film, notebook." Nadine scooped
her hair away from her face and retied her ponytail
as she took a quick inventory, pencil stuck firmly in
her mouth. She looked up at Wally as he rubbed his
forehead, looking a little pale.

"I think I still got the flu," he mumbled.

"I thought you were finished with that."

"Maybe it was your article on Skyline that
brought it back on," he joked weakly.

Nadine didn't think that was funny. She and Clint
avoided each other, but the tension in the office between them was palpable.

Wally groaned again and doubled over. "I think
I better get back home," he said as he clutched his
stomach.

"Okay," she grumbled, annoyed at him for still
being sick, and feeling guilty at her reaction. "I'll
drop you off on my way. Can you make it to my
car?"

He nodded and slowly got up.

Nadine zipped her bag shut. "I need more film. I'll meet you outside."

Wally only groaned in reply and stumbled out the door. Nadine followed him down the hall, making a quick stop at the darkroom to grab her film.

As she closed the door behind her she met Clint walking up the hallway, a frown on his face. "What's with Wally?" he asked.

Nadine swallowed and willed her beating heart to slow down. This was the first time since yesterday morning that they had spoken. "The f-flu…I think," she stuttered.

"Didn't you need him today?" he asked with an impatient frown.

"I guess I'll have to do without him."

"You were headed out to the Foodgrains Project, weren't you?"

Nadine only nodded, wishing she could just leave. It was bad enough she had had moments of discomfort around Clint before the Skyline article. Since yesterday and her own awakening feelings, it was harder.

Clint tapped the sheaf of papers he was carrying, his lips pursed. "Do you want me to help out?" he asked, his voice casual.

Nadine's head shot up. Why would he want to come? "No, no," she said hurriedly. "I'd just as soon do it on my own."

Clint nodded and Nadine realized that it sounded as if she was brushing him off. Donna's reprimand warred with her own confusion around her boss as she forced a smile at him, and she amended her statement. "I mean…that's okay. I don't want to bother you. You've covered for Wally enough the past few days."

"I don't mind. I could stand to get out for a bit."

Nadine glanced at his clothes, and he looked down himself.

"Don't worry. I'll change," he said.

Nadine chewed her lip, wondering what it would be like to have him around an entire morning, wishing he'd be called to a sudden emergency. Then, feeling distinctly un-Christlike, she nodded. "Sure," she said, forcing a cheerful note into her voice.

"Okay." Clint nodded without smiling. "I'll meet you at Nanninga's quarter in about an hour."

Nadine's eyes met his and once again she felt a pull of attraction. Their gaze held and then she glanced away. "Sounds good," she said quietly, then turned and went out to her car where Wally was waiting.

Clint got to the town limits and pushed the accelerator on his sports car to the floor. He felt boyishly excited and knew he shouldn't. Nadine had made it fairly clear that she allowed his presence on sufferance. He wondered why he kept harboring some faint hope that she would soften toward him. Two things precluded that—her boyfriend and her opposing stance on Skyline. He had gone to her office on Tuesday morning hoping he could try yet once more to talk her out of the latter, and if not that, at least try to get her to tone down her rhetoric.

His partner had called today with predictable news. He had just come out of a meeting with Skyline's lawyers. Another lawsuit was pending.

The newspaper was making a comfortable living for all involved, but not a huge profit. And it got less with each court challenge Skyline mounted.

Nadine put him in an awkward situation. He lost no matter which way he turned.

Because for better or worse, he was unable to change his feelings for Nadine Laidlaw. Deep feelings. Serious feelings.

He had always been attracted to her, but she'd often made it fairly clear what she thought of him. However, she had slowly warmed to him the longer he went out with Sabrina. Though even after spending half an evening laughing and talking with him and her sisters, Nadine had always kept a reserve about her.

But lately he had caught a hint of vulnerability, a softening that drew him, made him want to peel away the sarcastic outer shell.

He knew what he would find beneath that. He read her articles, sensed her deep, unwavering faith, caught the wry humor that permeated her writing. When she wrote, she showed a side of herself that she seemed wary of showing to him.

Clint turned down the tree-lined driveway leading to his home and couldn't help but smile.

When he had moved here as a sullen teenager,

Uncle Dory had put him to work, planting, mowing, weeding and in general maintaining the large yard and surrounding pastures and outbuildings. Growing up in the city, he had never had to do any physical work.

His parents were both professionals who were never home, and when they were, they fought. Clint was an only child who had turned into an ornery teenager whom his parents didn't know how to handle. When he was caught shoplifting they shipped him off to Uncle Dory with the hope that this calm, straightforward man would be able to turn their son around. What Dory did was keep Clint very busy.

As well as three newspapers, Dory owned eighty acres, ten cows, three horses, chickens, rabbits, potbellied pigs and about six dogs. Clint was responsible for feeding and cleaning the barns and stalls.

In time he began to enjoy the horses nuzzling him as he doled out their grain ration, nickering to him when he came to fork hay for them. He began taking more time with his daily chores. Working with the animals brought about a sense of satisfaction that had been missing from Clint's life in the city.

He and his patient uncle worked well together. Soon Clint helped with other jobs. Together he and Uncle Dory finished renovating the comfortable story-and-a-half home, and Clint took as much pride in it then as he did now.

Clint slammed the door of the car and strode up the gravel path to the house. He skirted the bushes nestled against the front entrance and unlocked the heavy wooden door, then shed his suit jacket and loosened his tie as he ran up the carpeted stairs to his bedroom. He turned to his cupboard to dig out more suitable clothes for a trip to the harvest project.

Jeans, T-shirt and an old corduroy shirt that was a carryover from his backpacking days. He slipped on the worn clothes, feeling as if he was going back in time. He generally favored suits and a more formal look for work, completely opposite to his uncle. It was his way of making a statement. Ties and crisp monochrome shirts as opposed to the worn sweaters and corduroy pants of his uncle. Tight writing with newsworthy stories instead of breezy, loosely written articles that meandered all over the map.

And Clint had begun to put his own stamp on the newspaper. It took time to clean out the deadwood and make the changes, but on the whole things were going well. His biggest problem was also his biggest asset.

Nadine Laidlaw. His editor and, it seemed, constant critic.

He wished he could understand his changing feelings for her. He reminded himself that she had a boyfriend. Trace Bennet.

But for some reason that Clint couldn't pin down, he didn't quite trust Mr. Bennet. Jealousy, perhaps. Certainly a smoothness on Trace's part that he couldn't see Nadine being attracted to.

He wondered if he should just give up. But in his heart he knew he simply couldn't.

He dug through the cupboard for his own camera

and bag. Even though Nadine would be taking most of the pictures, he liked to keep his own skills up. He checked through it, making sure it was loaded, packed up some extra lenses, then slung it over his shoulder. He walked down the stairs, pausing at the bottom as he wondered once again, what had made him offer to help.

Was it her obvious frustration as she stood contemplating a sick reporter? The fact that she had been working extra hard the past few weeks covering for a reporter who had suddenly quit?

Or the notion of spending a morning with her away from the office and the politics of manager and editor?

Clint shook his head. It didn't matter. He had offered and now he was committed. If he had learned anything from his newfound faith, it was that there were times to work, times to pray and times to let things flow on their own.

Five combines lumbered down the field, the roar of the large diesel engines thundering through the peace of the surrounding countryside. Chopped straw spewed out of the back of the machines. Choking grain dust swirled upward and the sun shone like a benediction in a promising blue sky.

Nadine glanced once more over her shoulder at the gravel road, mentally calculating how long it would take Clint to get here.

The combines had already made one full round

and she was itching to go. She couldn't wait for him, and didn't want to admit that she was.

Finally she grabbed her camera bag and jumped out of her car, jogging over to one of the grain trucks that stood ready to relieve the combines of the harvest.

The driver was leaning against the truck. "You're from the paper, aren't you?" he asked, pulling on the bill of his cap.

Nadine nodded as she pulled her camera and light meter out. "And I'm going to take your picture." She took a quick reading, adjusted the settings on her camera, focused on the driver and snapped her first picture. Nadine guessed from the bright logo emblazoned on his obviously new cap that the hat had been a freebie from one of the various implement dealers in the area.

Trace's competition, she thought. Once more she wondered what had happened last night. Or for that matter, Sunday. He hadn't called to explain and she wasn't about to chase him down.

A small red car pulled in behind hers. She couldn't stop the gentle lift of her heart, and when Clint stepped out of the vehicle, it was as if time had turned back.

He wore a brown corduroy shirt that hung open over a plain white T-shirt. Jeans hugged his long legs and sneakers finished the look totally at odds with his usual tucked-in shirt and tie.

Nadine felt her heart slow, then begin a dangerous

thumping. He looked like the old Clint Fletcher she used to dream about.

He sauntered over, notebook and pen in one hand, his camera slung over his shoulder. The wind lifted his hair, softening it and making it fall carelessly over his forehead.

Nadine couldn't keep her eyes off him.

He stopped beside her. "How long ago did they begin?"

Nadine swallowed and returned her attention to her camera, fiddling uselessly with the lens. "Just started," she muttered.

She looked at the camera slung over his shoulder by its strap, and her discomfort made her take refuge in her usual caustic comments. "Took your own camera in case I muck up?"

Clint shook his head "It's just for myself."

Nadine opened her mouth to apologize, then looked up at his handsome features. A soft smile played around the corners of his mouth, making him even more attractive than usual, and she changed her mind. Her sarcasm was her only defense against him.

"I should get going. I just got here, and need to get some pictures. Haven't taken any yet....'' And now you're babbling, you ninny, she reprimanded herself. Just because he shows up dressed in jeans looking like the old Clint Fletcher doesn't mean you need to make a fool of yourself.

"Talk to you later," she said, then turned and ran down the field toward the combines, her heart banging against her chest. You idiot, she fumed, he's just Clint Fletcher, the man you love to torment. You don't need to torture yourself by falling for him all over again.

Nadine took a steadying breath and lifted the camera to her face. Five combines crested the hill, their bulky shapes silhouetted against the sharp blue sky. The thunder of their engines gave Nadine a thrill.

The combines roared toward her, gobbling up the thick, fragrant swaths that lay in readiness on the golden stubble. The grains of wheat spun through various screens inside the combines. The straw was spewed out the back, mulch for next year's crop. The wheat was stored in temporary bins inside the combine. Once they were full, the trucks would pull up alongside and the hopper of the combine would spill out its bounty in a fountain of grain destined for people who had so much less.

Behind the combine, the field looked swept clean. All that was left was stubble strewn with finely chopped straw, looking like a buzz cut on a young boy.

"He will clear his threshing floor, gathering his wheat..." The quote from Matthew came to mind as Nadine walked, staying just ahead of the massive machines lumbering down the field.

She had done a lot of harvest pictures over the past couple of weeks, but this particular annual harvest held a special place in her heart. The Food-grains Bank Project was a cooperative effort of the community. A large map of the quarter section or sections was displayed in the local co-op store and divided into parcels. Anyone who wished could purchase a parcel to help pay for the costs of seeding and fertilizing. The use of the land was donated, then the land was planted, sprayed for weeds and harvested by volunteers.

The grain went to Third World countries, where it was "paid" out in exchange for work from the people of the country they were assisting.

Nadine had done a piece on it each year since she first heard about it and felt as much a part of it as any of the organizers. She always bought her own acre and helped keep track of the progress of the combines, cheering when "her" part was done.

The Foodgrains Bank Project always had an air of celebration about it. Local implement dealers donated combines, members of the local church prepared a lunch for the volunteers. And some people came just to be spectators. The project became a way of recognizing the good things God had given the farming community around Derwin and a vehicle for farmers to share their harvest with much needier people.

One by one the five combines mowed down wide swaths of grain. Once filled, they spilled out the wheat, filling the huge truck. The truck pulled away and the combines returned to their swaths.

Nadine took many shots of the entire process. Then she glanced over at the group of people standing around the huge map of the quarter section. Clint was talking to a few of the volunteers, smiling, nodding. He held a cup of coffee, his notebook stuffed in his pocket, camera now hanging around his neck. Someone spoke. He laughed, his eyes bright, the deep timbre of his voice warming her soul like sunlight.

Nadine felt time still, pause and turn back. She hadn't seen this side of Clint since he had returned to Derwin a couple of months ago. Always he insisted on a measure of aloofness, always he held his emotions in reserve. But the Clint who mingled and mixed with the group of people on the edge of the field was so much like the Clint who had lived in Derwin those many years ago that her step faltered in reaction.

She was falling for him all over again.

She knew that as a Christian woman she could find contentment in service, in the myriad of things the church offered. She knew that serving the Lord should be her first priority.

But now, as she saw Clint, she realized yet again that a gaping emptiness in her life remained. It didn't matter how many lectures on the joys of single life she attended, or how many times she read the apostle Paul's passage on being unmarried, she still struggled with a need for human contact—and affection. For someone's eyes to light up when they saw her, for someone to miss her when she was gone. A parting kiss in the morning, a hand to take her own as she walked down the street.

Nadine squinted at the men standing against the

white grain box of the truck, their multicolored hats a bright contrast. It would be a tricky shot with the sun glaring off the white background. She raised the camera, analyzing the composition with one part of her mind even as the other tried to analyze her own life.

It was self-preservation that kept Trace at a distance, she concluded, snapping a few pictures, zooming in closer. It was the same thing that kept her sniping at Clint Fletcher. Trace she let get a bit close because she knew she could deal with him.

Clint was another story.

Nadine repressed her thoughts, concentrating on her job. She moved the camera along the group of men. They were the implement dealers and would appreciate having their picture in the paper, so she got a few more frames of them.

Then she stopped as Clint's face came into view. Nadine held her camera steady, unable to move it on. She adjusted the zoom, pulling the picture in, adjusting the focus. Clint's mouth was curved in a crooked smile, his eyes squinting against the bright sun. A soft breeze teased his hair, softened its usual crisp style. Unable to stop herself, Nadine snapped a few pictures. Then he turned her way and through the eye of the camera she saw him look at her, his gaze so intent, it seemed as if he was directly in front of her instead of fifty feet away.

Nadine felt her breath slow. She lowered the camera, still looking at him. Then she turned away and with shaking hands wound the film, wondering if the pictures would even turn out.

Nadine had intended to spend about an hour there, but was chivied by the organizers into staying for lunch.

"There's more than enough," said Freda Harper, wife of one of the implement dealers. She almost pulled Nadine over to the table that was set up in the shade of a grain truck. "Besides, I understand elk burgers are on the menu."

"Sounds intriguing." Nadine felt her stomach clench with hunger as she caught a whiff of the food on the barbecue. She glanced over the table spread with salads, buns, a few vegetable platters and squares. "And it sure looks good."

"Well, dish up." Freda smiled at Nadine as she helped herself to some potato salad. "We've had such a beautiful fall," Freda continued as she worked her way down the table. "I'm so glad the weatherman co-operated today, too."

"It sure has been a blessing for all the farmers," replied Nadine with a smile.

Freda nodded, her red hair glinting in the sun, a bright contrast to the yellow sweatshirt she wore, then leaned closer. "You know, I've always meant to write you a letter, but I'm not much for doing that." She smiled apologetically. "But I've always wanted to say that I sure appreciate all the support you give this project. Douglas, my husband, got involved because of an article you wrote. How it's a chance for us, who have so much, to share." Freda scooped up a spoonful of salad and paused a moment. "But even more than that, I appreciate the way you always bring your faith out in the editorials you write. It's very encouraging to other Christians." Freda stopped, as if slightly embarrassed by her admission. "Anyhow, thanks."

Nadine felt a spiral of warmth curl up her heart. "Thank you," she said. Freda Harper's encouraging words were a gentle reminder to Nadine that her job was important and that it was used by God. "That's good to know. I guess it's one of the few places that I express my own faith."

Freda grinned back at her. "I imagine it's a little harder to show it in volleyball scores and hockey summaries."

"Your daughter plays volleyball, doesn't she?"

Freda nodded, and the talk moved to sports and children. Nadine found out that Freda had two girls in volleyball, one in senior high, one in junior high. They also had one foster child and one adopted child. The Harpers were a giving, loving family and Nadine had lots of questions for Freda.

By the time they got to the end of the line, they were chatting as if they had known each other much longer than the ten minutes they had spent together, and Nadine's busy reporter's mind had another idea for a feature article.

Chapter Eight

"**S**orry Nadine, but I told you I was stuck in a meeting...."

Nadine tried to smile. "You have quite a few meetings, Trace."

"It's this new business. It's a lot of work to set up."

"Whatever." Nadine tucked the phone under her ear and squatted by her filing cabinet. She tugged it open with an angry jerk.

"Really, Nadine. I'm not trying to put you on. I'm going to be in town in the morning. Can I come then?"

"No. I've got to interview a reporter for the opening here."

"What about Thursday night?" She hesitated, not entirely sure she wanted to chance another date with Trace.

"C'mon," he said, his voice wheedling. "Don't make me suffer."

"Why do I have such a hard time believing you?"

"Nadine. I really wanted to come last night."

Still she hesitated, unable to shake the feeling that he had been avoiding her.

"Once things slow down, I'll have way more time. I've got a few loose ends to tie up, and once that happens, I'm all yours. You have to believe me."

Nadine didn't know if she was imagining the pleading tone of his voice, but he sounded genuinely upset. She thought of Clint and the time they had spent together today. Going out with Trace would give her the emotional distance she needed from Clint. Trace was becoming less important to her, while she knew what she felt for Clint could hurt her more in the long run. "We'll aim for tomorrow night," she said with a sigh. Would she regret this? she wondered.

"Great, that's just great," he enthused. "I'll pick you up at five o'clock. I can hardly wait to see you."

She fiddled with the phone cord, frustrated with herself for her wavering attitude. "I'll see you tomorrow, then, Trace."

"For sure, Nadine. I won't let you down."

"I hope not," Nadine said. She ended the call and dropped the phone in the cradle, pulling a face at it as she did so. My life and welcome to it, she thought.

With a shake of her head, Nadine picked up some papers from the desk and shoved them into the appropriate folder in the file cabinet. She was acting in such a typically feminine fashion, even if she didn't dress the part. She glanced down at the blue jeans she wore today—and most every day. Running her finger over them, she remembered Clint's reaction when she'd worn a skirt. Remembered the surprised look on his face, the way his eyes had seemed to linger.

So different from his usual penetrating look. When he dropped that aloof manner, his eyes could sparkle, his usually firm mouth would soften and he was suddenly charming, infinitely appealing.

She called back this morning, how the wind had teased the groomed line of his hair, how his eyes had crinkled up as he smiled. Her hands dangled uselessly between the file folders as she relived each time their gazes had locked, each time they'd seemed to make a connection.

The tinny ring of the phone broke into her thoughts and Nadine pulled herself up short, mentally giving herself a shake. What in the world was wrong with her? she wondered. Getting all dreamy over Clint Fletcher.

She was losing it, she thought as she got up and picked up the phone. "Hello," she said curtly, pushing shut the door of the filing cabinet with her foot.

"Is this Nadine Laidlaw?" a harsh voice asked on the other end of the phone.

"Yes." Nadine frowned as she tried to place the caller.

"I sent you a letter. The one about Skyline. Did you get it?"

Nadine felt her own breath leave her as she fumbled behind her for a chair. "Okay. I remember now. You said you knew something and wanted to talk to me."

"I can't tell you over the phone. I want to meet you somewhere. Are you going to be at the volleyball tournament next week?"

Nadine hoped a new reporter would be hired by then and the new person would cover the game. But she couldn't chance this. Not after all this time. She had to meet this woman wherever and whenever she asked. "If you are talking about the one at the high school, the answer is yes." She scribbled a note on a pad, her hands shaking.

"Good. I have a son on the team. I'll be there."

"And who is this?"

"It doesn't matter." The woman sighed. "It doesn't matter who I am. I'll be wearing a green sweatshirt and gray pants." A pause. "I don't want to do this, but I really have to."

Nadine swallowed, her own heart pounding with a mixture of excitement and fear. "I'm glad. I'm glad you're willing to talk to me." Nadine wiped a damp hand on the leg of her jeans. "I'll see you at the tournament, then."

A sharp click in her ear signaled the end of the conversation. Nadine slowly replaced the handset, her heart refusing to slow down, her thoughts spinning. Six years she had speculated on the circumstances surrounding her father's death. Six years she had asked questions and received no answers.

And now.

Now she was so close, so close.

Thank you, Lord, she prayed, clasping her hands in front of her mouth to stop the trembling of her lips. *Thank you for keeping faith. Thank you that I will finally be able to bring that company to justice.* The thought might be premature, but she felt a deep conviction that now, finally, she would find out the truth.

"And the truth shall make you free."

It was what Nadine had been striving for. She longed to be finished with the struggle. While as her grandmother and Donna chided her for her near obsession with Skyline, a small part of her knew they were correct. She had prayed, grappled with the comfort offered her in the Bible. Even while her mother was alive there were many times she had been tempted to quit, let it all go and realize there were going to be questions that would just not be answered. Then she would come home or visit her mother in the hospital. Brenda would be lying in her bed, barely able to speak, but always able to make it understood that she wouldn't have peace until Skyline was exposed.

Once she talked to her mysterious tipper, she might discover something she could work into an article. She knew Clint would hit the roof. She didn't want to deliberately antagonize him, but she knew this letter and the new information was a chance for her to assuage the guilt that clung at each thought of her mother's death.

But for now, she had pictures to develop and a few articles to write up.

Nadine reached over and unzipped her camera bag, pulling out the rolls of exposed film. If she didn't develop the pictures now, her time would get eaten up with phone calls and paperwork. She gathered up the film and walked down the hallway.

She knocked on the darkroom door. No one replied, so she pushed the heavy door open. Stepping inside, she closed it right away, giving her eyes a chance to adjust to the darkness. It was supposed to be absolute, but she was blessed with good night vision and could make out the vague outline of the workbench and sinks. She had spent countless hours in here when she first started, fascinated with the procedure of developing film. Thankfully this was one place Clint had not changed. Things were in exactly the same place they always had been. She walked slowly over to the bench and found the equipment she needed. With quick, sure movements she laid out her rolls of film and pried up the tops of the canisters with an old can opener, careful not to dent them too much. They were reusable and could be filled again. Using her memory of the room, she easily located the plastic developing reels and with quick movements worked the exposed film onto the reels and readied the graduates that would hold the film and developing liquid. These she filled with developer and then carefully lowered the reels into the containers. Snapping the lid on, she began slowly agitating them, inverting them repeatedly for the first thirty seconds.

She had about ten seconds to go on this stage of the developing when she heard a hesitant tap at the door.

"It's okay to come in, but do it quickly," Nadine called over her shoulder. She agitated the graduates one last time, wondering who else wanted to use the darkroom. The door opened and was quickly shut again. "Be warned," she said. "You're stuck in here until I'm done." She poured the developer into the sink, rinsed the graduates and snapped the lid back on. She switched on the red light above the counter and measured the stop bath into the container.

"That's okay," an all-too-familiar voice replied. Clint.

Nadine swallowed and clutched the containers to stop the sudden trembling of her fingers. "What..." She swallowed and started again. "What do you want?"

"I had some film to develop."

With a flick of her hand Nadine switched off the red light. She opened the graduates and poured the stop bath over the negatives and snapped the lid on. She felt, more than heard, Clint walk over to the sink beside her. In the dark her other senses became heightened. She could hear his breathing, sense his presence. His proximity gave her a sudden jitter. Her heart beat heavily at the base of her throat. She agitated the containers, reminding herself to move slowly. After dumping out the stop bath, she poured the fixative onto the film and reached for the timer again. As she did so her arm brushed against Clint's.

"Sorry," she mumbled, finding the timer, only to drop it on the floor. Chiding herself for her clumsiness, she bent over trying to find it.

She felt the timer, but as she reached to pick it up, she felt other fingers encircle hers. Startled, she almost dropped the mechanism again, but Clint's hand held hers and the metal clock.

Nadine's hand refused to respond. She felt the warmth of Clint's fingers covering hers as his other hand gently took the clock away from her.

"How long should I set it for?" he asked.

Nadine told him, then took a hurried step away from him and the feelings he generated in her. She didn't want to be so aware of him. She didn't want Clint, of all people, to have that kind of control over her. *I don't want this to happen, Lord,* she prayed fervently. One deep breath, then another and thankfully, she felt her equilibrium returning.

But she could stay in the one small corner of the darkroom for only a couple of minutes. She had to finish the last stage.

Thankfully Clint had moved and she could grab the canister and retreat to the opposite counter.

The silence in the room grew with each minute the timer ticked off, each "swish" of the developing tank. Nadine felt she should say something, anything, but it was as if her mind had shut off.

She could hear by his movements that Clint was finished rolling his film onto the developing reels. He would have to wait until the timer was finished to immerse his film in solution, and Nadine mentally hurried the minutes on.

"I thought today went well," Clint said, breaking the silence that seemed even more intense in the small, dark space.

"Yes, it did."

"You're keeping quite late hours today, aren't you?"

"Have to." Her voice sounded small in the darkness; his seemed to take it over.

"I imagine your grandma will be waiting."

"Yes." Brilliant conversation, Nadine, she scolded herself, trying to come up with anything that she could say to him.

"She's quite the go-getter."

"She can be a little overwhelming."

"She was always really friendly when I came over," Clint said quietly.

"Yes, she was." Nadine almost groaned at her lame response, resisting the urge to smack herself on the forehead. What's the matter? she thought. You spend the morning with him, then he corners you in the darkroom, tosses a few lame questions at you and you freeze up.

But even as she formulated the thought, she knew why. It had to do with the daydreaming she had indulged in a few moments ago in her office, with seeing him all morning. It had to do with a sudden and unwelcome awareness of Clint as an attractive man. It had to do with old emotions and old feelings. With new emotions, too. And she didn't like it.

The silence lengthened. Then Clint cleared his throat. "I never did give you proper condolences with the death of your mother. I can tell it's been hard for you."

Once again Nadine felt her chest tighten as still-painful emotions clenched her heart. She nodded, then, realizing he couldn't see the movement of her head, said softly, "Yes it has." She sniffed and reached into her pocket for a tissue, but her pocket was empty.

"Are you okay?" Clint's voice was a soft, rich sound, disembodied in the darkness.

"Yes." She wrapped her arms around her stomach, simply allowing the tears to fall unheeded down her cheeks. She ceased caring. Clint couldn't see her, anyway.

Through the darkness, she could make out Clint's tall figure taking a step closer. His hand reached out as if to find her. Nadine couldn't move, didn't want to. Then warm fingers lightly touched her cheek. A rustling sound, and once again he was carefully wiping her eyes with a handkerchief.

Nadine felt her stomach drop, her heart slow. She could feel his breath on her hair, the warmth of his fingers through the thin material of his handkerchief. She wanted him to stop. She wanted him to continue. She felt herself swaying toward him, was aware of every movement he made. It was as if an uncontrolled magnetism slowly drew them closer...closer. His breath was on her face now, her mouth. She tilted her head up toward him, feeling more than seeing his presence, and slowly their lips touched with tender hesitancy.

The clang of the timer shattered the moment. Nadine jumped and pulled back.

"I've got to get my film out of the solution. It's...ready...." Nadine turned away from him, her heart pounding. Fumbling with the containers, she yanked the tops off. She rinsed the negatives, her hands shaking, and soon had the strips of film hanging up to dry from the line strung along one end of the darkroom. Then she whisked the residual moisture off them with her fingers, not bothering to get a squeegee. All she wanted now was to finish and get out. After rinsing her hands under the tap, she quickly stepped to the door.

"Let me know when I can open the door, please," she asked Clint, her voice breathless.

"Sure," he answered, his tone brusque.

Nadine could hardly wait until he told her she could go, unable to speculate on what he had done— and her response. When he finally gave her leave, she tugged on the doorknob, and when she was out into the bright light of the office, she felt like a prisoner escaping. For a moment she stood by the darkroom door, catching her breath. Don't be silly, she chided herself. Clint was her boss. All he did was...

Touch her face with his hard, strong fingers. Wipe her tears...

An unwelcome weakness pervaded her limbs as she remembered again his gentle touch, his nearness. How tempted she had been to drift against him, to be enfolded against that broad chest, to close her eyes as he'd kissed her.

Nadine allowed herself one moment of fantasy, a few seconds of daydreaming. Then with a short laugh she returned to reality.

She was Nadine Laidlaw. Editor of the *Derwin Times*. She was attaching too much importance to a few moments of sympathy.

She was supposed to be dating Trace Bennet. Had a date with him tomorrow night, in fact.

But for a reason she didn't want to examine, she hoped he wouldn't show.

"The job is yours if you want it." Nadine smiled at the young girl sitting across the desk from her.

Allison Edlinger grinned, leaning forward, her long blond hair slipping over her shoulder. "This is great. Just great. Thanks so much. When can I start?"

"Yesterday?" Nadine joked at Allison's enthusiasm. There had been six applicants for the job and only two were interview material. Of the two, Allison had the more impressive credentials—three summers' work for a weekly paper in southern Alberta and two years at another. Nadine had also been impressed by Allison's clips. "Actually, you can start as soon as possible. We've been just swamped." Nadine indicated her desk, which was full again in spite of a few long evenings. "If you want, I can show you around today. We've got deadline on Monday. Our paper comes out on Tuesday."

"That's a little unusual for a weekly," Allison commented.

"Yes. Most come out on Monday, but our new general manager changed the date so that we didn't have to work Sunday anymore. At least, not as much."

Nadine rose and ushered Allison out of her office. They walked to the back of the building where the two typesetters worked at their computers. She poked her head over Wally's cubicle on the other side of the large, open room, but he was gone. "This is where you'll be working," Nadine said, pointing to the cubicle that abutted Wally's.

They walked past the darkroom and Nadine introduced Allison to Cory, whose office was across the hallway.

"Cory is our ad person. She usually words the ads, helps set them out," Nadine said, indicating the older woman. They walked past Nadine's own office, and Donna's across from hers was also empty. "Empty building today," Nadine commented as they walked to the reception area. Nadine leaned on the counter. "And this is Sharlene, our receptionist, ad taker, sometimes copy editor..."

"Date with Trace tonight?" quipped Sharlene,

reaching across to rearrange a fold of Nadine's scarf, which draped across her brown blazer.

"I guess we'll see. We were supposed to go out a couple of nights ago, but he cried off."

Nadine pushed away from the desk and walked over to Clint's office, effectively cutting off conversation with Sharlene. She felt uncomfortable talking about Trace. She had told herself she had dressed up for her date, but she was secretly hoping Clint was around, as well.

Nadine turned and gestured to the door that faced the open foyer. "And this, Allison, is our boss's office. Thankfully he's gone for the day, so I'll just let you have a peek into the inner sanctum."

Nadine opened the door.

"No, he's not—" Sharlene interrupted, but she was too late.

Nadine almost jumped at the sight of Clint working at his desk. He looked up and Nadine backed away. "Sorry. I was just showing our new reporter around." She reached over to close the door, but Clint was getting up from his desk.

"It's okay."

"I d-didn't want to interrupt you," Nadine stammered, suddenly feeling self-conscious of her skirt, her hair, her makeup. She remembered all too vividly the time spent together at the harvest and the episode in the darkroom.

"It doesn't matter," he said, glancing at Nadine, his eyes flicking over her clothes, a smile curving his mouth. "I wouldn't mind meeting her."

Of course he wanted to meet a new hire. How dumb of her. Nadine stepped back, taking a breath to compose herself.

Nadine made the introductions, and Clint reached out to shake Allison's hand. Allison smiled up at him, her blue eyes shining with appreciation. It seemed to Nadine that the light from the front windows caught Allison's blond hair, making it sparkle. Her dress emphasized her delicate shoulders and skimmed her narrow hips.

"Allison is starting today," Nadine announced, her voice sounding falsely bright. "She's originally from Vancouver, but has lived here for a couple of years already."

Clint glanced at Nadine, acknowledging her comment with a hesitant smile, then looked back at Allison. "Nice to have you with us, Allison. I hope you'll be working with us for a while."

Allison fairly simpered, and Nadine resisted the urge to roll her eyes. "I hope so, too," she said almost coyly.

"We should go back to my office," Nadine said to Allison. "There's a few things I want to go over with you—camera allowance, travel, that kind of thing. And then Donna will need you for the payroll forms."

It looked to Nadine as if Allison had to tear her gaze away from Clint's. "Sure," Allison said vaguely. "We can do that." She hesitated a moment, then followed Nadine back down the hall. When she opened the door to her office, Nadine was not surprised to see Clint still standing in the doorway of his office, watching them.

Always was partial to blondes, she thought as she closed the door behind Allison.

Nadine walked around her desk and slipped into her chair, pulled an empty pad of paper toward her and found a pen that still wrote. "First I need to get your address and phone number."

Allison said nothing and Nadine looked up.

"Earth to Allison."

Allison jumped. "I am so sorry," she apologized. "I have to confess that I'm still a little surprised."

"At what?" As if she didn't know, but politeness dictated that she had to ask.

"At how handsome the boss is." Allison shook her head as if she was still trying to absorb it. "He's so good-looking, and what dreamy eyes."

Nadine stopped, her pen poised over the pad of paper. "He *is* your boss, I'd like to remind you," she said, her tone more sharp than she had intended.

Allison sighed, then smiled at Nadine. "Sorry. I didn't mean to sound like some drippy teenager, but I sure never imagined meeting someone like him in a town like this."

"Well, these unfortunate incidents happen," replied Nadine dryly. "Now. I'd really like to get on with this."

Someone rapped abruptly on her door and Cory stuck her head in. "Accident just came in on the scanner. Truck rolled over on the highway."

"Where's Wally?"

"Can't raise him on his cell phone. I'm pretty sure he's at the opening of the museum."

Nadine jumped up and grabbed her camera bag, checking it for the necessary supplies. She glanced at Allison. "Well, are you ready for your first assignment?"

Allison looked surprised, then nodded. "Sure."

"Great." Nadine looked back up at Cory as she zipped up her bag. "Where are we headed?"

"Secondary highway, 498, north toward Riverview."

"Leaving now. Any more info on who's involved?" Nadine asked as Cory stepped quickly aside for her.

"The trucker involved..." Cory hesitated as Nadine headed out the doorway. Nadine stopped and glanced over her shoulder.

"What?"

Cory bit her lip. "He was working for Skyline."

Chapter Nine

"**I** couldn't believe how ticked that one guy was when you started taking pictures," Allison said to Nadine as they returned to the office. "I thought he was going to pull your camera out of your hand."

"There's more to that story," Nadine said grimly, stopping at the darkroom. She was surprised herself at how quickly some of the administrative people from Skyline had come to the scene of the accident. Nadine got some pictures of the paramedics working on the injured truck driver before she was blocked by the workers from Skyline.

"I'm going to have to wait and see what happens to him before we run these pictures, though," Nadine continued, dropping the canisters on the counter. "We have a standing rule not to print pictures of actual fatalities. If he doesn't make it, we're going to have to make an editorial decision as to which pictures we'll run."

"I'd say run the ones of the Skyline people trying to block the picture," Allison said as they walked out of the darkroom, stopping at Nadine's office.

"Not a bad idea." Nadine glanced at her watch. "I guess you've just put your first day's work in." She smiled up at Allison. "Do you have a place to stay for the night, or are you going to go back home?"

Allison shrugged. "I'm staying at a friend's tonight. She promised she would help me find an apartment if I got the job."

"Looks like you'll be hunting." Nadine let her camera bag drop to the floor. "You'll be covering a livestock show in Eastbar in the afternoon. I suggest pants."

Allison looked down at her dress. "We sure looked a pair, rushing out of your car, both of us dressed to the nines." She glanced at Nadine's legs. "I don't know how you managed to keep your hose from running."

"Me neither," confessed Nadine. She had discovered that she liked Allison. She was helpful, enthusiastic and a good sport. It hadn't taken her long to figure out what she needed to do at the accident scene. Her guileless smile and breezy manner had caught a lot of people off guard and they were, therefore, more forthcoming to her than they ever would have been to Nadine. "Just as well. I'm supposed to be going on a date tonight."

Allison frowned. "If you'll excuse me, you don't sound too enthusiastic."

"Probably not," she admitted.

"I'd ditch him and make a play for the boss," Allison said with a grin. "I haven't been here long, but if a guy looked at me like he looks at you, I wouldn't waste my time on someone I didn't like."

"Time out," Nadine said firmly. "First of all, he's your boss and *mine* and secondly, Clint Fletcher looks at me like he'd like to fire me but doesn't know how."

"Sorry," Allison said, suddenly contrite. "I didn't realize you felt that way about him."

"I don't feel any 'way.' I see him as my employer, and that is the only relationship we have." And don't we sound prim, Nadine thought.

"I'm sorry. Not exactly a good footing to start out on, is it?"

"No, I'm sorry," Nadine reassured her, frustrated with her lapse. "I always get uptight after covering an accident." Nadine glanced at her watch. "Well, I have to do some work yet and you should head out to your friend's place." She looked back at Allison and held out her hand. "Thanks again. I think it will be a good article."

Allison smiled in relief and shook Nadine's hand. "I hope so. And thanks again for the job." She tucked her notebook in her purse, turned and walked down the hall, her blond hair swinging with each step.

Nadine watched her go. So Allison thought Clint looked at her a special way. Did he really?

Nadine shook off the thought and went into her

office. Pulling her chair up to her desk, she flipped through a pile of message slips and began answering them.

A while later she had finished up the calls and she turned her computer on, ostensibly to work on a story, but instead she ended up playing a computer game. Entirely appropriate, she thought. Once again, it's just me and my computer.

With a sigh, she clicked the Close button, jabbed at the power button on the monitor with one finger and the tower with another. The screen flicked off and the fan on the computer died down, leaving the office in total silence.

Trace had told her he would pick her up at five. The last time Nadine had checked her watch, it had been five-thirty. She refused to look at it again.

She lifted her bag onto the desk, shoved some papers into it that she would look over at home and zipped the bag shut, gritting her teeth as she felt the unwelcome and all-too-familiar prickling in her eyes. She had never been the weepy type, but since her mother died, her emotions were so close to the surface. Tonight was nothing to cry over, she castigated herself. Trace isn't that important to you.

But it seemed that she was crying more and more and she disliked it intensely each time it happened.

Except once, she thought. In the darkroom. When Clint had dried her tears.

Nadine felt her stomach clench at the remembrance of Clint's hands on her face, his gentle comfort. For a brief moment she allowed herself the luxury of remembering his touch, the scent of his aftershave, his hovering nearness.

Then with an angry shake of her head she dismissed the memories. He felt sorry for her and had said as much before he dried her tears.

Nadine hefted her bag onto her shoulder and got ready to leave, yet hesitated as she turned the doorknob.

Going home meant Grandma and her unsubtle "I told you so" looks. It would be too humiliating to have Grandma see her come home from another canceled date.

So then what? Another solitary movie in Eastbar had no appeal, and eating alone had even less.

Nadine dropped her bag in frustration and started unbuttoning her blazer. She wouldn't go out by herself, yet she wanted her grandma out of her house. She wanted to be alone and when she had the chance, she felt lonely.

Wishy-washy. That was what she was, she thought as she hung her blazer over the back of her chair. She was easily pushed around and easily taken in. Trace was a case in point. How many dates had he kept as opposed to the ones he had broken?

Not that it mattered that much, Nadine thought, dropping into her chair. She had felt uncomfortable with Trace from the start. The whole relationship was contrived, almost like an arranged marriage.

Trace wasn't important to her. She still felt uneasy about him. Something about their relationship just didn't seem right. Yet, in a way she was loath to call it off altogether. What would she have then?

And what do you have now? she reminded herself, rocking back in her chair. You're all alone in this office. You were supposed to go out with him. Nadine blew her breath out in a sigh and pushed her chair away from her desk. She didn't feel like writing up the Skyline story and didn't want to go home.

She got up and wandered around the deserted office. Even Clint was gone. The thought made her feel unaccountably lonely.

Each step seemed to drag, each step echoing in the empty building as if mocking her own lonely state.

I've tried, Lord, she prayed, stepping into her small office. *I've tried to be happy with what I have. What's wrong with me?*

Wasn't she supposed to be a liberated woman? Hadn't she shown that she could compete with a man, could do the same job? Wasn't that supposed to be enough for a woman these days?

Nadine sat in her chair, letting her head fall backward, her eyes close. Deep down she wanted what her friends had. A husband, children. A home. She wanted to sit in church and frown at fidgeting kids, sing with her husband. She wanted to have windows to sew curtains for, laundry to wash. She wanted a house with an office that she could work out of, parttime. She wanted to hear a door open and close, feel a lift of her heart as her husband came into the house, feel the same sense of completion she had felt when her own father would come home and fill up the man-space that had been empty since he had left that morning. And she wanted that man to be Clint.

And who did she think she was fooling? she thought, frustrated with where her own thoughts so easily went. She remembered all too well the contrast between her and Allison this morning, how Clint couldn't seem to keep his eyes off the blonde.

Clint wasn't for her. Nadine figured she was destined to become one of those old newspaper ladies who ended up heading out to South America doing features on Mayan temples for travel magazines.

Or maybe a dedicated single missionary who would work in faraway mission fields. Then come back and do church tours and slide shows, drumming up support for evangelism in exotic locales far away.

With a wry smile at the mental picture, Nadine bent over, pulled open one of her drawers and found her Bible.

It had been a long time since she had read it at work. In the early days, shortly after her father died and her mother became ill, Nadine kept one Bible at work, one at home. She read both frequently, drinking from the well that never ran dry. She needed God so much then. Needed answers to questions that she couldn't seem to puzzle out on her own.

Each day had begun with reading and prayer...then.

And now?

Lately she felt events slipping out of her reach, deadlines always looming. They had been short-handed too long and it had drained her.

The sorrow she felt at her mother's death was still too fresh, and her guilt over being unable to find more about her father's death still haunted her.

Nadine pressed her hand against her chest as if to keep the sorrow contained. She pulled the Bible out of the drawer and laid it on her desk.

She drew in a deep breath, then another. God had answered her scattered prayers about her father. God had been faithful. The phone call yesterday was confirmation to her that she was given another chance.

Nadine opened the Bible, leafing through the worn book, margins marked with notations from various Bible studies. Almost lazily she flipped through pages. "Grazing," her mother used to call it almost contemptuously. Brenda, in true accordance with her own strict upbringing, had insisted that the Bible be read from front to back.

It was thanks to this disciplined reading that Nadine had worked her way a number of times through the entire Bible. She had learned to appreciate the sorrows of the prophets watching their people turn away from God, to lament with them at the hardness of hearts.

But when her own heart was sore, when her own anger seemed to overwhelm her, she found herself turning to either the Psalms or the letters Paul wrote in the New Testament. It was there she found comfort for her anguish, balm for her sorrow and reminders to forgive.

But tonight she felt like lamenting, and turned to Isaiah.

She flipped through the chapters, reading imprecations of woe to those who turned away and yet finding at the same time the promises that Isaiah gave of the comforter.

Isaiah 55.

Nadine stopped, carefully running her fingers along the familiar lines. "Come all who are thirsty, come to the waters.... Why spend money on what is not bread and your labor on what does not satisfy?... Seek the Lord while He may be found.... You will go out with joy and be led forth with peace." As she read, the words slowly wound themselves around her worn and weary heart and she laid the book open on her desktop, hunching over it much as a cold person would over a glowing fire. Drawing in a slow breath, she read on, reading warnings and comfort and promises.

After reading for a while, Nadine bent her head in prayer, asking for wisdom and discernment and strength. She knew she didn't have to count on the men of the world for her happiness. God would give her what she needed.

Encouraged, Nadine slowly closed the Bible and placed it on one corner of her desk, ready for tomorrow.

Smiling lightly, she pulled her blazer off the back of her chair and slipped it on. With her scarf draped around her neck, she was ready to walk out of the office when the phone rang.

For a moment she was tempted to let it ring, but her innate curiosity led her back to her desk to answer it.

Trace was full of apologies and promises to come over right away, but Nadine cut him off. "Doesn't matter, Trace. It's over." As she spoke the words she felt a momentary shaft of panic. Was she crazy? Was she deliberately trying to sabotage any chance she would have at a life's partner?

But as she heard his protests, listened to his excuses, she realized that the longer she allowed the relationship to go on the worse it would get. Trace simply wasn't reliable, wasn't the kind of man she wanted for herself.

"No. I've thought it over," she interrupted. "You're just too busy and I don't like being stood up."

"Nadine, don't do this. Tonight was a blip, unexpected."

"Like your visit with your banker?" Nadine put heavy emphasis on the last word as if to tell him that she didn't believe his excuse of the other day, either.

"Her name is Margaret Toornstra. Give her a call." Nadine heard him take a breath, then another as if he was running. "Please, don't do this, Nadine. I'm begging you."

Nadine had heard his begging before and found it a little embarrassing. But she knew she had to end it. If she was to have a meaningful relationship, she wanted it with someone dependable and trustworthy.

If she was to have a relationship. She closed her eyes as the words taunted and echoed in her mind. She knew she had to trust. Being married wasn't everything. She had a challenging job and lived in a good place. She had her faith and her church community. As lonely as she sometimes felt, she wasn't desperate enough to settle for a man who showed her such little respect. She respected herself far too much for that.

She listened to more of his protests, his promises, waiting for a suitable time to end the conversation. It was a relief when she could finally say, "Goodbye, Trace," and hang up the phone.

As she did so, she shook her head. For a brief moment she felt a pang of sorrow, but then, behind that, a feeling of empowerment. She, plain ordinary Nadine Laidlaw, single woman of twenty-seven, had broken up with a very handsome, eligible man. She had made the choice, no one else.

And that thought, more than anything else, put a smile on her lips.

She walked down the hallway toward the front of the office. She might regret the impulse in the morning, but for tonight she felt as if she was in charge. She turned on the security, locked the main office door, then went back down the hallway to the back of the building turning lights off as she went.

Maybe Grandma would have some fresh muffins

made, Nadine thought as she pulled out the keys to her car. To sweeten her I-told-you-so's.

Headlights swung down the alley and momentarily blinded her. Nadine stepped back toward the newspaper office. A car pulled up beside hers, and with a start, Nadine recognized Clint's vehicle.

The car stopped and Clint got out, walking around to meet her. "Hi, there," he said. "Going out?"

Nadine shook her head, a sense of shame mocking her newfound confidence. "No, just home."

"But I thought you had a date...."

"I did." Nadine shrugged, fully aware of her boss standing beside her, his height overwhelming her. His hair looked tousled, and his tie was gone, causing Nadine to recall the way he'd looked the day they'd covered the Foodgrains Project together.

"And..." he prompted, "he broke it?"

Nadine shook her head, fiddling with the end of her scarf. "No. I did. I didn't feel like waiting anymore." She looked up at him, only to catch his gaze on her. She looked down again. "What are you doing here?"

"Forgot some papers I needed." He jingled the change in his pants pocket. "So what are you going to do?"

Nadine shrugged. "Go home. See if Grandma has any supper left for me."

"I see." He made a move to leave, checked himself and came back. "I, uh..." He stopped and cleared his throat. Nadine glanced up at him, puzzled. He seemed hesitant, unsure of himself. "I haven't eaten, either. We could grab a bite at the inn."

Nadine paused in surprise, her hands no longer fiddling with her scarf. "Okay," she agreed, hardly knowing what else to say.

"Good." Clint took a step backward and whacked his leg against the fender of his car. He steadied himself, straightened and held his hand up to Nadine. "Sorry."

She didn't know what he was apologizing for, but his unexpected—and uncharacteristic—clumsiness gave him a sudden vulnerability.

"So. Do you want to ride with me or take your car?"

"I'll drive my car." She wanted the option of being able to leave on her own. "I'll meet you there."

He nodded, took another step back. "Okay. I'll see you later." He turned and jogged up the walk to the office, leaving Nadine to wonder what had come over her usually calm and collected boss.

Briefly she recalled his touch yesterday, his concern. Then with a laugh she dismissed her foolish thoughts. He just wanted company and she just happened to be handy.

But as she backed out of the parking lot behind the *Derwin Times,* she couldn't help remembering his grin when she'd said yes.

Clint settled himself behind the table and glanced across it to where Nadine sat. Her gaze roved around the restaurant, as she looked everywhere but at him. For a moment he regretted asking her. She seemed ill at ease, even though she had agreed to come.

He couldn't get her off his mind lately. It seemed that each day he tried to seek her out, tried to find out where she was.

That moment in the darkroom when he had kissed her. He still didn't know what had come over him. She had a boyfriend.

The guy who had stood her up tonight.

Clint took the menu from the smiling waitress and looked once again at Nadine.

Her thick brown hair shone with reddish highlights and hung loose, framing her face, softening her features even though tonight she looked a little tense.

Not at all unusual, he reflected. Nadine never seemed comfortable whenever he was around. And that in turn created a measure of tension within him. He didn't like it. He wanted her to be as relaxed around him as she had been around the people the afternoon of the Foodgrains Project. He wanted her to look up at him with a smile brightening her eyes, the way it had that day.

"What are you going to have?" she asked.

He wasn't really hungry, and had asked Nadine out for supper on an impulse. He had two issues to confront with her, and he guessed she would dislike dealing with one as much as the other.

One had to do with his changing feelings toward her. The other with Skyline. And for the first time in his life he didn't know how to proceed with either.

"The chicken burger and potato salad," he told the waitress, handing back the menu.

Nadine smiled at him. "Sounds like a good balance between health and convenience."

Clint just nodded, his heart skipping a beat at the sight of the smile he had wished for.

"I'll have a bowl of beef barley soup." She laid her menu down and folded her hands on the table in front of her. "Not really hungry," she explained, tapping her thumbs against each other, then looking around the restaurant.

They sat in a strained silence until the waitress left, and then Clint knew it would be up to him.

"How are your sisters?" Not that he really cared, but he had to start the conversation somehow.

Nadine smiled. "Fine. I haven't been to see Sabrina's daughter for a couple of weeks, but she's cute. Leslie is also expecting a baby."

"Wow." He shook his head. "Seems hard to imagine either of them married."

Nadine tilted her head in acknowledgment, glancing at him, then away. "I always knew both of them would get married before I did."

Clint didn't know if he imagined the hint of pain in her voice and wondered if she was jealous. "Why did you know that?"

"You of all people can answer that." She lifted her eyebrows at him. "After all, you went out with one of them."

But really only wanted to be with you, he thought. He was quickly losing ground with her. He needed to change the subject, and grasped at the first thing that came to mind. "How long was your mother sick?"

Nadine pursed her lips, picking up her napkin, playing with it. "Most ALS sufferers live anywhere from one to three years after diagnosis. In mother's case it took a little longer."

"How come?"

Nadine carefully pleated the napkin as if weighing her answer. Then she looked up at him, holding his gaze. "My mother's mission kept her alive longer. And that mission was to see Skyline Contractors brought to justice for my father's death." Nadine stopped abruptly and bit her lip.

Clint absorbed this piece of news with a heavy heart. How could he do what he had to after what she had just told him?

He reminded himself that he was her boss, that his partner was practically screaming at him to rein her in. That another lawsuit would cost too much and that this time Skyline would do more than threaten.

"I know that your father died while working for Skyline, but I've never heard how it happened." Even as he spoke the words Clint wondered if he was fashioning his own noose. But he wanted to know. Wanted to find out what it was that drove her to keep up the battle after all these years. Wanted to discover what he could about her.

"Didn't Sabrina tell you?"

"She only told me that he died at work."

"Do you want to hear the official line we got, or do you want to hear what I think?" She looked away, then at him, her expression troubled.

"Tell me both." He leaned forward, wishing he could forget about his paper, wishing he dared give in to a sudden and intense need to protect her, to support her.

She carefully unfolded the napkin again. "The line we got from the company was that my father was out in the bush by himself. He was using a felling practice calling domino falling. What you essentially do is drop one tree so that it hangs up on another, cut that tree until it leans against another and so on. Then you get one main tree that falls all the way, taking all the others with it. It's highly illegal according to labor standards and extremely dangerous. Lots of fallers get killed that way. According to Skyline, this is what my father did, and he was killed by a hung-up tree coming down on him." Nadine stared up at Clint, her brown eyes intense. "My father was the most careful man I know. He would never do anything as dangerous as that."

"So what do you think happened?"

Nadine held his gaze a moment, then looked down again. "That's what I've been trying to find out. I've talked to as many employees that will talk to me, other subcontractors. I've heard rumors that my father went in behind another young guy to clean up the mess he made. I've heard that he was working in tandem with another faller. And I've heard that it was just fluke.'' Nadine held up one hand, ticking off her fingers with the other. ''I haven't gotten any names, any times, any sign of other vehicles, no verification of any of the rumors, at least not anyone who was willing to commit. Nothing.''

''The bush is a pretty wild place.''

Nadine almost laughed. ''Not when there's a logging show or two in an area. You go out there, it's like a little community. If my mom wanted to bring my dad supper, and we made a wrong turn, all we'd have to do is drive until we saw a skidder or Cat operator. They always knew who was working where. But in my father's case…nothing.''

Clint didn't know what to say. Nadine's voice took on a note of authority that showed him clearly that she knew of what she spoke, and how important it was to her.

''How did you find out?''

''My father didn't come home that night and my mother called my dad's supervisor. He went back to the bush looking for my father. It took a while because he wasn't working in the block he had been assigned to. At least, not according to the supervisor's information.'' Nadine folded the napkin again, her eyes intently focused on it. ''He was found lying underneath a tree. Dead.''

Clint gave in to a sudden impulse. He reached across the table and covered her hands with his, squeezing them, wanting to pull her close, to comfort her. "You must have cared for him a lot."

Nadine looked down at their hands and tightened her grip on his. "I did. I loved him a lot." She bit her lip, but when she looked back up at him, her eyes were clear but pensive. "Seems kind of wrong," she said with a soft laugh. "I had my mother around longer than my father, but sometimes it's as if I miss him more." She shrugged, then pulled her hands away from him.

"Your mother was a lot of work for you and your grandmother, wasn't she?"

Nadine waved the comment away with a graceful turn of her hand. "I resented it at first, but then I wondered if it wasn't God's way of giving me a chance to get to know her better. I always spent so much time with my dad." She smiled, her eyes looking over his shoulder as if she had disappeared into another place and time. "We would go out to the bush on Saturdays to cut firewood. The other girls stayed at home with mom." She smiled softly. "He called me his little tomboy." She shook her head and looked back at Clint.

"I always remember him as a very kind man." Clint folded his arms, leaning his elbows on the table. "He would always ask about Uncle Dory and what we were working on at the acreage."

"He liked you."

"I liked him. He was a man of integrity who was content with his life." Clint couldn't keep the bitter note out of his voice. "Unlike so many others."

"Others being…" prompted Nadine.

Clint rubbed his thumb along the inside of his opposite arm, concentrating on the tabletop. "My parents."

"And…" Nadine prompted. "What about *your* parents."

Clint shrugged, hesitant to tell her even after all these years. "They both worked very hard to collect enough money to buy more things. They were going to give me a car when I graduated high school."

"But you didn't get it."

"No. I blew it. That's how I ended up at Dory's. I was caught stealing a flashlight from a hardware store." He looked up at her, his mouth curved in a wry grin. "My parents didn't understand what was happening. Neither did I."

"You wanted them to notice you."

Clint caught Nadine's intent look, surprised at her expression. As if she had just discovered something new, and, he conceded, she probably had. At that time he hadn't told too many people how he had ended up in Derwin. It was embarrassing to admit to anyone he wanted to impress that he had only stolen a flashlight. As he got to know the Laidlaws he said nothing—more because of his shame over the ease with which his parents had sent him away that far out shadowed any guilt he felt over a mistake. "That's exactly what Uncle Dory said," he said softly.

"And where are your parents now?"

"Dad's in Rome and Mother shuttles between To-

ronto and New York.'' Clint smiled at her as if to
negate the bitterness that crept into his voice. He
had forgiven his parents the same time he had become a Christian, but he still struggled with it.

''I take it they're divorced.''

''You take it correctly.''

''But it still bothers you.''

Clint lifted one shoulder in a negligent shrug. ''It
doesn't matter what the marriage counselors say, it's
always hard on kids when their family breaks up.
At any age.'' Clint looked back up at Nadine, pleas-
antly surprised to see a gentle understanding in her
expression. ''Your family was one of the first ones
I saw that worked. A family that cared about each
other. A family that loved God. I've always wanted
that for myself.''

Nadine looked down and Clint thought that
maybe he had overstepped some unknown bound-
ary. One never knew with Nadine and he had been
talking more in the past few minutes than he had in
days.

But the moment was interrupted as the waitress
returned with their order. She laid the plates down
in front of them. Clint smiled his thanks at her.

The waitress left and Clint hesitated and then,
without looking at Nadine, bent his head to say
grace. He raised his head precisely the same time as
Nadine. Their eyes met and held, a feeling of accord
springing up between them.

It felt right to be sitting across a table from her,

to say grace together. To be joined in a communion of spirit and mind.

Clint smiled carefully at her and when she returned that smile, he felt his heart lift.

He winged another silent prayer heavenward. A quick prayer for patience on his part and understanding on hers.

He just wished for exactly the right moment to bring up what he knew he had to talk to her about.

Chapter Ten

Nadine stirred her soup, trying to adjust to her new feelings about Clint. She felt as if all her defenses against this man had suddenly melted away, and she wanted to know as much as she could.

She glanced up at him, surprised yet again to see his eyes on her. Looking down, she busied herself with unwrapping her cracker from its cellophane wrapper. "When you left Derwin you went to Europe, didn't you?" As if she didn't know. Against her own will she had known every movement he made, thanks both to Sabrina and her own unquenchable interest in his whereabouts.

"My parents had a collective attack of guilt over their divorce, and sending me away on that trip was their way of making up for it."

Nadine felt her cheeks warm, remembering all too well a snide comment she had made in this very place when she had sat here with Trace.

"That trip was one of the really good things that happened to me." Clint was quiet a moment, his finger tracing idle circles on the tablecloth, his supper forgotten. "I traveled through places of extreme wealth and extreme poverty. I learned that what had happened to me was fairly small in the larger scheme of things. I stopped in churches that were older than any book I had read, I visited castles and museums and toured countryside that had been home to generations of families. And in a busy square in Jerusalem it was as if all the history I had seen in Europe, everything I had witnessed with your family, the myriad times I had sat in church with Uncle Dory and even my own parents, all coalesced. I realized that I had been given a precious gift not only of life, but of death. Christ's death. And that people all over the world and all through history had believed that and clung to it through all the happenings of their life." Clint looked up at her, his mouth quirked in a gentle smile. "I changed, I accepted all those promises that had been handed to me in so many ways. And then I had to come home." He hesitated a moment, as if he wanted to say more and was unsure of how to proceed.

Their waitress came by asking if either of them wanted more coffee. Nadine nodded and held out her cup, as did Clint.

When she left, Nadine leaned forward, full of questions, yet unsure of where to go. Clint's confession had created a sudden openness, a place to begin to get to know each other in new ways. He

told her more of Europe, spoke of his work in the
city and of his desire to one day come back to Derwin and take over his uncle's paper. A desire that
had begun as a random thought and had changed
into a real need as his own life changed.

The waitress had taken their plates and bowls
away and poured another round of coffee. Clint
leaned his elbows on the table, sipping as he asked
her questions, responding easily to hers.

She idly fiddled with her spoon, answering his
own soft-spoken questions, telling him about the
precious few things that had happened in her life
since he had left Derwin. A few times she glanced
up at him to find him looking at her, his expression
serious.

At those moments she felt her own heart quicken.

It wasn't until their waitress had come around for
the fifth or sixth time with coffee that she realized
how long they had sat there. She snuck a quick
glance at her watch.

"My goodness," she exclaimed aloud. "It's
eleven o'clock."

Clint frowned as if disbelieving her. He glanced
at his own wrist. "You're right." He looked up at
her and smiled. "I can't believe we've been sitting
here that long."

Neither could Nadine. "I should get going.
Grandma will be worried."

"But you were supposed to be out tonight anyway, weren't you?"

"Yes, but I never liked to stay out too long. I usually made Trace take me home before ten."

"Well, then, we had better leave." Clint pulled a few dollars out of his pocket for a tip and dropped them on the table. He also took the check before Nadine had a chance. "I'll get it," he said in reply to her protest. "I've never had a chance to take you out and have often wanted to." He winked at her and got up. "Be back in a minute." Bemused at his parting comment—and his wink—Nadine watched him walk confidently across the deserted restaurant.

She gathered her discarded scarf, purse and knapsack and got up herself, following more slowly, wondering what he meant, and wondering if she was reading more into the casual comment than he implied. By the time she came to the front desk, he was pocketing his wallet and turning back to the dining room.

"I'd offer to drive you home, but I imagine you'll want to take your car home?"

Nadine nodded, sorry now that she had taken it, wondering what would have transpired if he had driven her home. "Thanks so much for dinner," she said, pulling her keys out of her purse.

Clint nodded, then, walking ahead, he opened the heavy glass door for her. They walked in silence through the parking lot to her car. Nadine fumbled through her purse for her keys. When she finally found them, she felt awkward and foolish.

"Here, let me," Clint said softly, taking the keys out of her hand. He opened the door and helped

Nadine into the car. He held the keys, studying them. The lights of the parking lot cast his face in shadows. All evening he had looked relaxed and comfortable, drawing her out, smiling. But now his lips were clamped together, and a frown drew his dark eyebrows together.

"Nadine, I need to ask you something."

Here it comes, she thought. The real reason he asked me out. "Go ahead."

He took a deep breath. "I understand that you covered the accident at Skyline."

"What about it?" She stiffened in reaction, afraid of his answer, his somber tone.

He held on to the door and looked away, as if unable to face her. "I would like it if you could assign the story to Wally. Or better yet, Allison."

Nadine closed her eyes and resisted the urge to cry, scream, anything. You naive child, she chastised herself. This was why he asked you out. How could you think that Clint Fletcher would, for one minute, forget his precious newspaper?

"Can I ask why?" she said, her voice low, controlled.

"Objectivity."

"Which you don't think I have."

Clint shook his head. "I think you're too close to it, emotionally."

"Which you conveniently found out tonight," she said sharply. "It would have been cheaper for you to just tell me tomorrow at the office." She held out her hand for her keys. Why are you doing this? a more objective part of her mind cried out. Relax. Talk to him. But echoes of her own insecurity seemed to drown out common sense.

"You don't need to put yourself through all those emotions of your father's death again."

"Spare me the false concern," she said angrily, reaching up to take the keys from his unresisting fingers. "I've been a reporter long enough. I know how to cover a story."

Heartsore and angry, she gave the door a tug and managed to pull it away from him this time. She started the car, gunned the engine, reversed out of the space and tore out of the parking lot. The streetlights flashed past the window, blurred by her tears. She palmed them away as she steered her car past familiar houses and streets.

She hit the brakes and rocked to a halt in front of her apartment, then dropped her head on the steering wheel. Don't you dare cry, she told herself.

But somehow part of her didn't heed the voice, and the tears that slid down her face were hot with recrimination and sorrow.

Nadine booted up her office computer, pulled out her keyboard and, once she got into the office's word processing program, opened the Skyline folder.

She had been on the phone all morning and had a stack of notes from Allison as well as the pictures. This time she had made contact prints, or proofs, of the negatives. The story was too important to leave to chance and she wanted exactly the right shot.

She rearranged the hastily scribbled notes on one side of the U-shaped computer desk, reviewing the information that she had just about committed to memory.

As Nadine wrote up the story, weaving in the statistics, one part of her mind analyzed the flow, the other kept her emotions in check with difficulty. She had to prove to Clint that she could write this story objectively.

She was immersed in her work when she heard a tap at the door. "Come in," she called out without looking up.

"What's up, Allison?" she mumbled, pulling a pencil from behind her ear. She marked off one of the papers and turned back to the screen.

She frowned, her fingers flying over the keyboard. She was about to hit the backspace key to correct an error when she realized that whoever had come into the office still had said nothing. She glanced over her shoulder, and found her vision blocked by an expanse of white shirt, bisected by a brown tie.

Flustered, she turned back to the screen, conscious of Clint's hovering presence behind her. Her fingers stilled and she could say nothing, all too aware of what had happened last night.

He still said nothing. Instead she saw his hands come down on either side of her computer desk, surrounding her as he read over her shoulder. She could feel the faint warmth of his breath on her neck, could feel his presence around her, behind her, above her.

What was he trying to do? Intimidate her? Frighten her?

Taking a steadying breath, she typed a few more words. She tried to keep her eyes straight ahead and away from his large hands on either side of her, but she couldn't. Her fingers slowed.

"Please, Clint," she said, her voice breathless, "if you're trying to intimidate me, you're succeeding."

Her hands froze on the keyboard as she felt his chin lightly brush the top of her head. "What do you want?" she asked finally.

"I don't know," he replied, his throaty voice soft in her ear.

Nadine swallowed as her breathing sped up, her heart in sync. She could feel the warmth of his body behind her. He was close enough that all she had to do was lean her head back and she would touch him.

"Please stop doing this." She had no defenses against him. He had been too much a part of her daydreams, her longings, and she didn't know anymore where one left off and the other began.

He moved one hand, his weight shifted and Nadine thought he was going to straighten. Instead she felt his fingers lightly brush her hair aside, sending shivers skittering down her spine. And then, impossibly, she felt warm, soft lips touch her neck. They lingered a moment, their touch weakening her. She couldn't move, couldn't breathe, wished he would continue, prayed he would stop.

"Nadine," he whispered against her neck, his breath caressing it with a soft warmth. Then, finally, he straightened. He lightly touched her hair. "I need to talk to you...." His voice was subdued. Nadine bit her lip, half turning toward him, her vulnerability there for him to see.

The sharp ring of the phone broke the moment. Sharlene's voice came over the intercom. "Trace is on line one for you, Nadine." The door burst open and Donna strode in carrying a pile of computer printouts that Nadine had requested.

Nadine pressed her hand against her face, confusion warring with a hysterical urge to laugh. She hit the button that connected her to Sharlene's speaker phone. "I don't want to talk to him," she said sharply.

"Sure, hon." Sharlene broke off the connection.

Nadine turned to Clint, ignoring Donna, who stood in front of her desk, holding out the papers for Nadine to take. But Clint was already backing out the door, his eyes on hers, his face mirroring the confusion in Nadine's.

Why was he leaving? What did he mean by what he had done? Nadine followed Clint's exit with her eyes, still ignoring Donna. Finally she pulled herself together and took the documents from her.

"What did Clint want?" Donna asked. "You look like you're in shock."

"I am," she said in a faraway voice, her fingers

brushing over the place where he had, just seconds ago, kissed her. She shook her head and, ignoring Donna's curious stare, dropped the papers on her desk and turned back to her computer, trying to collect her thoughts, her wits and all the other things Clint had scattered with his casual caress.

"So what happened?" Donna asked, leaning on Nadine's desk as if to get a closer look at her friend.

Nadine only shook her head. "I don't want to talk about it."

"You look like you should."

Nadine tried to type a few more words, then stopped and turned. "Clint...he just came in here...I think he wanted to talk." Nadine lifted her hands helplessly and shrugged.

"He looked about as stunned as you did. What happened between you two?"

What indeed, thought Nadine. She could still feel the soft warmth of his lips on her neck, hear the tenderness in his voice as he spoke her name.

"Earth to Nadine. Come in, *please.*"

Nadine jumped at the sight of Donna's hand waving in front of her face. "Sorry." Flustered, she turned back to her computer, unwilling to face her friend's curious gaze. "I...don't want to talk right now."

"Sure," Donna straightened. "If you want to come over tonight and tell me then, we're doing the usual Friday-night thing," she offered as she backed out of the office.

Nadine nodded and smiled her thanks. Donna was

a true friend. Knew when to ask questions and when to back off.

When the door closed she looked back at the screen, trying to read the words she had typed just moments ago, trying to understand what she had said.

But she might as well have been reading Chinese. She let her eyes close, her hands idle on the keyboard. In the space of a day she felt as if her entire world had rearranged. Yesterday at this time she was contemplating a date with Trace. Now...

Trace was out of the picture and Clint had taken her out and, today, had kissed her.

And that gentle caress had moved her more profoundly than anything that had happened to her before. What was he trying to do? Was this just another way of getting her to change her mind? Would Clint resort to such measures just to keep his paper safe?

Even as she asked the questions, she knew that more was going on between them than manipulation.

Clint carefully closed the door to his office behind him, leaned back against the wall and dragged his hands over his face, wondering what had come over him.

He had gone into Nadine's office hoping to talk to her about a compromise regarding Skyline. But when he entered her office and saw her, it was as if something else moved his feet, his hands. He started reading over her shoulder, remembered what she had told him yesterday, heard the puzzled sorrow, felt her anguish at the loss of her father. Then suddenly he didn't want to talk anymore.

Clint shook his head. He was acting like a high school kid. He had a paper to run. He couldn't afford to get Skyline's back up. He knew they had to run the article, but what he had read on Nadine's computer did not bode well for her emotional detachment.

The anger that flowed from her fingers into the article had as much to do with her own unfinished sorrow as the recent accident that, he had found out, was not Skyline's fault. The trucker was a subcontractor and therefore responsible for his own equipment and his own hours.

Ten minutes ago he had received this information from an old friend who worked with the trucker. The friend hadn't wanted to talk to Nadine about the accident because he was afraid it would come back to Skyline and he would lose his own contract with them.

But how could Clint tell her this without making it look as if he was on Skyline's side, which he wasn't? His friend had told him enough that Clint himself could fill an entire newspaper with stories of graft, misappropriated government funds and fudged records. Only, no one would willingly confirm what he said. Jobs were scarce right now. No one was willing to put their paycheck or contracts in jeopardy.

And to top it off, his partner had phoned him early this morning, reading out a letter from Skyline informing their publishing group of an intent to sue should any more defamatory articles show up in the newspaper on Tuesday. He was leaving first thing Monday for Calgary. Which meant he had today and the weekend to either tone down Nadine's crusade or get someone else to write the article.

Clint walked slowly over to his desk. He was stuck no matter which way he turned. If he let Nadine write what it looked as if she was going to, they would get sued for sure. If he asked her once again to back off, he knew she would freeze him out just as she had yesterday evening.

Clint sat in his chair, rested his elbows on his desk, dropped his face into his hands.

Okay, Lord, he prayed, *show me what to do with Nadine. Show me how to manage this paper so that You are shown to a world. Help me balance what I want with what I need. Show me what to do with Nadine, Skyline, my work.* He prayed to let go, to trust that God would provide him with what he needed.

He wanted Nadine, he wanted his newspaper, and unless things changed, he wasn't about to get both.

Nadine rolled over and glanced idly at the clock by her bed. He heart plunged. Eight in the morning! In a panic, she shoved the tangle of blankets aside. She was supposed to cover the high school volleyball tournament in Edmonton in half an hour.

Nadine stopped herself midstride, and with a satisfied smile crawled back into bed.

She had forgotten about Allison Edlinger, their new reporter. She would be doing the sports beat from now on.

Nadine snuggled farther into the covers, relishing the fact that she could lie there for another hour if she wanted.

She hadn't told Grandma about her breakup with Trace, and there was no way she'd tell her about her dinner with Clint.

Sunday came with a sudden drop in temperature. Nadine spent an extra half hour in an agony of indecision choosing what to wear, how to do her hair, what to say when she saw Clint again, what he would say, but to no avail. Clint wasn't in church. The heaviness of disappointment wouldn't ease. Back at home, Nadine prowled around the apartment, restless and uneasy, all the while berating herself for acting like a teenager in the throes of a crush. By afternoon she changed into blue jeans and a sweater and retreated to her bedroom-cum-office. Once there she pulled up the Skyline file. She hadn't gotten anywhere the day before, and the story would have to be done by Monday morning to be able to be put in place in the paper. She had it in mind for a front-page story, though she knew Clint wanted it second or third page.

She could give in on that, she conceded as she pulled up the file.

Ignoring the guilt that accompanied working on Sunday, she typed a few words, deleted them, rearranged some of the copy, but it didn't seem to help. Somehow the words sounded stilted, harsh. She didn't know if it was Clint's words haunting her, or reality.

Had she lost her objectivity in regard to Skyline?

Frustrated, she fiddled with the words again. Nothing would come. She decided to check some of the previous stories, to see what she'd done with them.

A few clicks got her into her Skyline folder and then into all of the previous stories.

She highlighted them and opened them all at once. The first one came up on top and Nadine skimmed it, trying to read her reporting from a third-party point of view. It was easier to do now, this many years after the fact.

It had been written five years ago, a year after her father died and she had started working at the paper. She wrinkled her nose at the setup, the flow of the story. Obviously written shortly after her one term of journalism school.

And obviously written from the perspective of a very angry and bitter young woman. Nadine sighed as she read through it, realizing how this must look to Clint and anyone else who read it. Long words, lots of rhetoric and sprinkled with exclamation marks. With a click of her mouse button she closed it and skimmed through the next one and then the next.

Clint was right. Her emotions had guided her writing. When she compared it to other stories she had done, the Skyline articles held a measure of shrillness.

On a hunch, she printed them all out, including her most recent story, and brought them to her grandmother, who sat on the couch knitting socks, humming along with the CD of hymns playing softly on the stereo.

"Can you do me a favor, Grandma?" Nadine asked, handing her the rough draft of her most recent article. "Can you read this and tell me what you think?"

Danielle took the paper and slipped on the reading glasses hanging from a delicate chain around her neck. When she was finished she looked at Nadine, then back at the paper.

"Tell me the truth, Grandma," Nadine urged, sitting down on the couch beside her.

Danielle pursed her lips, glanced over it again and then handed it back to Nadine. "It sounds very angry. You make it look like the accident is all Skyline's fault, without coming right out and saying that, of course."

Nadine bit back a rebuttal. She had asked for an objective statement and she had gotten it. That her grandmother's words mirrored so closely what Clint had said was not collusion or a conspiracy.

"Okay. What about these?" Nadine handed her a few of the other articles she had written. "These are some old articles I've written over the years."

Danielle looked them over as well, her frown deepening with each one. "Funny that I don't remember reading them." Danielle shook her head and pushed her glasses up her nose again as she continued. The room was silent except for the rustling of papers as Grandma laid each one down beside her. When she was finished, she looked up at Nadine. "Why did you want me to read these?"

"I wanted a second opinion." She looked away, choosing her words carefully. "Clint is having trouble with Skyline Contractors. In the past few years, each time I've written an article about them, they've threaten to sue us."

Danielle gasped. "What? I don't remember reading anything about it in the 'Court Docket.'"

Nadine resisted the urge to laugh. "It wouldn't end up in there, Grandma. That's for minor stuff. The major stuff gets handled very neatly and tidily between lawyers who charge an arm and a leg to write threatening letters and file important documents back and forth." She picked up the articles, riffling through them absently. "They always threaten, but never follow through. The trouble is that it costs the newspaper each time this happens."

"And this latest story…"

"Is newsworthy. I don't know if they'd sue over it."

"So why did you want me to read it?"

"Because I wanted to know if my boss was right." Nadine hesitated. It was difficult to admit that she might have been wrong. "I wanted to know if I've let my emotions rule my reason."

"I think where Skyline is concerned, you have never been able to be completely objective." She stopped, picking up her knitting again.

"And..." prompted Nadine.

Danielle finished off the stitches on the needle and lowered the sock to her lap. "I know there was more to the story of your father's death than what we were told. There was never a more careful and cautious boy than Jake Laidlaw. When that—" Grandma pursed her lips angrily "—that slimy little man came to the door, trying to tell me that my son had done something unsafe and illegal..." Danielle glared at Nadine. "I was ready to go into battle. To prove them wrong. And I know you felt the same."

Nadine nodded, surprised at this side of her dear Grandma. Meddling, yes, but confrontational?

"But," Danielle continued, picking up her knitting again, "going into battle wouldn't bring your father back, trite as that may sound. Perhaps it was God's will. No one can say for sure." Danielle knit a few more stitches, her needles flashing. "Your mother wasn't content to let things lie. She fought, battled, argued, spent hours on the telephone. When she got sick, she needed someone to continue, to be her hands and eyes, and the job fell to you." Danielle paused, frowning at her needles. "I think your mother filled you with anger toward this company." Danielle looked up at her granddaughter with a sad smile. "I think your mother took all the anger from her grief and poured it into you. I know you had your own anger, but you have never been one to mope and feel sorry for yourself.'' Danielle shook her head. ''Your dear mother had a tendency to cling to righteous wrath. And when I read these pieces, I hear her anger, feel her pain.'' Danielle reached over and squeezed Nadine's shoulder. ''I want to know, too, the circumstances surrounding my son's death. But it happened six years ago, Nadine. I've seen you spend a lot of time on the phone, writing letters to the government, talking to government officials, the police, other Skyline workers. It was easing off just before your mother died, but I sense that you think you've failed her by not finding out after all this time.'' Danielle slid over and slipped an arm around Nadine's waist. ''Don't take on a burden that isn't yours to carry. You really have to let God take care of this one. Let Him comfort you, let Him carry that weight.''

Nadine closed her eyes and let her grandmother hug her. At the moment, Nadine felt as if Danielle Laidlaw was taller and stronger than she could ever hope to be.

She straightened and picked up the papers. Shuffling them into a neat pile, she stared at them without really seeing them. ''Was I wrong, Grandma? Was I wrong to write this? Was this a wrong thing to do?''

''I don't think so, dear.'' Danielle patted her on the shoulder. ''You are a very good writer, very eloquent and very emotional.''

Nadine laughed shortly.

"I think it might be wrong to have kept your anger going so long." Danielle stroked Nadine's hair tenderly. "You are a wonderful, caring girl. I've never heard you complain, or grumble, even though I know you've had to carry some heavy burdens." Danielle smiled at her granddaughter. "I've always been proud of what you have done in your life. Proud of the things you write, the way your faith shines in your stories and articles. Maybe what you need to do is read over what you have written once again, for yourself, and see if what you know of God's love is shown in these articles."

Nadine nodded, realizing that no matter how much she thought she knew, she could always learn something from her dear grandmother.

Her grandmother stroked her hand carefully. "But more than that I want to say that I love you, Nadine."

Nadine looked at her grandmother and caught her soft, wrinkled hand in hers, pressing it to her cheek. "I love you, too, Grandma. I love you, too."

Chapter Eleven

Nadine gathered up her papers, stood and bent over to drop a kiss on her grandmother's head. "Thanks, Grandma," she said softly as she straightened. Her fingers feathered over her grandmother's gray head affectionately and, smiling, she turned and walked down the hallway.

Inside her bedroom she stopped beside the computer, tapping the sheaf of papers against the top of her desk, chewing her lip. She still had all her notes at the office. Most of the groundwork had been done. The story had to be told.

But not by me, she reasoned, looking down at the articles she had poured so much emotion into. Too much emotion. Her grandmother was right.

Allison could do it. It would be a good lesson in working under the pressure of a deadline.

Nadine dropped into her chair, pulled out the keyboard and with a few quick strokes, deleted the story she had just finished. For a moment she stared at the white screen, wondering what she had just done.

As the cursor blinked silently back at her, she sat back, a sigh lifting her shoulders and dropping the weight she had been carrying since she had first heard of the accident a couple of days ago. Her anger had been ignited, and all the stories of Skyline's misdeeds had swirled around her head. She wanted to right what she saw as a wrong.

But now it was as if the anger had been swept away, the burning need she felt to see justice done quenched under a blanket of peace that surrounded her. She bent her head, her fingers pressed against her face.

Thank you, Lord, she prayed softly, *thank you for my grandmother and what she teaches me, thank you for my job and what I can do in it. Help me to make wise decisions. In all of my life.*

Then, as she lifted her eyes, she felt a smile tease her lips. It was going to be all right. She knew she didn't need to be the one to personally see that Skyline was brought to justice as she remembered a poem that Grandma was fond of quoting: "Though the mills of God grind slowly, yet they grind exceeding small;/Though with patience He stands waiting, with exactness grinds He all."

She didn't need to wield her words to take on what God could easily do himself and in his own time.

Nadine got up and stood by the window, her hands in her pockets as she stared out at the darkened street. The town looked exactly the same as it had a few minutes ago, but now it seemed to Nadine that she could look at it with more benevolent eyes.

A car drove slowly down the street, its headlights swinging around as it turned into their driveway. Puzzled, Nadine leaned closer, drawing aside the light curtain to see who it could be.

The car stopped and the driver got out. Trace.

What was he doing here? What did he want?

She dropped the curtain and, turning, ran out of her room, determined to get to the door before Grandma. But as she got to the kitchen, she realized she still wasn't as fast as her grandmother.

"Come in, Trace," Grandma was saying. "I'll tell Nadine you're here."

I should have told her, thought Nadine, but now it was too late.

She stepped into the kitchen just as Grandma came in from the entrance. "Oh, there you are, Nadine. Trace is here." Grandma wasn't smiling and neither was Nadine. No help for it, she thought. She was going to have to do this with witnesses.

"Hi, Nadine." Trace stood framed by the kitchen door, his eyes on her. He held out his hand as Nadine unconsciously stepped back. "You left this behind a couple of days ago," he said, showing her a cellular phone. "I thought I would return it."

"Thanks," Nadine said, reaching past her grandmother to take it from him. "I was wondering where it was."

Trace glanced over at Danielle, but when she

made no move to leave, he squared his shoulders and faced Nadine. "I'm really sorry about the other night."

Nadine shook her head. "Don't bother, Trace," she replied. "We don't have anything to say to each other."

"But we do. I need to talk to you. I have something to tell you that changes everything." Trace plunged his hand through his hair, his expression pleading. "Please, Nadine. I was hoping to come to church this morning and then come here after, but something came up."

As it always did, thought Nadine.

"Please come with me. Please hear me out," he continued.

Nadine didn't answer, but she suspected that if she didn't go with Trace he wouldn't leave until she heard what he had to say. And she didn't want to cause a scene in front of her grandma. She turned to Danielle. "I'm going with Trace for a short drive." She put heavy emphasis on the word *short*. "I'll be back in a while."

Her grandmother frowned up at her, as if questioning her wisdom, but Nadine shook her head.

As she walked past Trace, she caught a coat off a hook in the entrance and stepped out the door before he could open it for her. She was at his car before she realized she still carried her cell phone. Shoving it in the pocket of her jacket, she opened the car door and got in.

Trace started the car and drove slowly down the

street. In the dim glow of the streetlights Nadine could see that he hadn't shaved, his face looked haggard, heavy shadows circled his eyes.

"Where are we going?" she asked as he turned left toward the highway instead of right toward downtown.

"I just want to get away from town, just go for a drive," he replied. "I have a lot to tell you."

"Can you start?"

Trace glanced at her, biting his lip. "I don't know where to."

She frowned at that. "What do you mean?"

Once he turned onto the highway, he sped up. The lights of town receded behind them and Nadine felt a moment's apprehension. Trace seemed distraught, and she wondered at the wisdom of going with him in his car.

"I've had a lot on my mind lately," Trace said after a while. "I've had to make some hard decisions and I haven't been able to tell you about them." He looked at her again, reaching out for her hand.

But Nadine shook her head and kept her fingers wrapped around her jacket. A week ago she would have responded, but that was before Clint had comforted her, had taken her out, had been there when Trace wasn't.

Had kissed her.

"What haven't you been able to tell me about, Trace?" she asked.

Trace hesitated, his hands wrapped tightly around

the steering wheel. "When we met, there was an emptiness in my life that I couldn't fill."

His words echoed thoughts that had tortured Nadine as well, and for the first time since he had started the car, she looked at him fully.

He glanced at her and smiled carefully. "I really care for you, Nadine. I do. I've never met anyone like you, someone I could laugh with..." He paused and looked ahead again. "Someone who has a strong faith. Someone I could admire and love."

"But..." she prompted, sensing that there was much more that needed to be said.

Trace shook his head as if to deny what he had to do. "I'm married."

Married. She had been going out with a married man, spending time with him, laughing with him, keeping him away from a wife, maybe even children. "How..." she began, then stopped, unable to articulate her confusion, her anger. "How could you do this?" she whispered, clenching her jacket. "Why didn't you tell me?"

"My wife and I have been living apart for a few months already." Trace laughed shortly. "I had left Tina a couple of months earlier and moved into a hotel in Derwin. I started buying the paper regularly, and would read your articles. I could tell that you had a strong faith, that you had a strength that I was looking for. When I read the article about us I knew I had to come to the office. Then when I saw you sitting there, I was stunned. You were, are..." he corrected "so beautiful."

"Why were you and your wife separated?" Nadine interrupted him.

"Tina and I are incompatible. She didn't want to go to church and I did. She didn't want to raise our children to go, either...."

"You have children?" Nadine asked weakly. She dropped her head against the back of the seat, a nausea filling her stomach. How could he not tell her?

"That's why I haven't always been able to keep our dates. 'Cause of my kids. But it's not as bad as it looks," he continued hastily. "I'm getting a divorce. I'm going to try for custody of the children. Tina and I have already been living apart. I came to Derwin to make a new start, and then I met you." He sped up. "Can't you see? It was meant to be."

"No, it wasn't," she said vehemently. "It was a very bad mistake." Nadine felt like screaming. "You have a wife, children..." She couldn't get past that. "You went out with me when you should have been with them..." Nadine couldn't continue, couldn't think. "Turn around," she said suddenly.

"Nadine, you don't understand. I did visit them when I wanted to be with you. But once the divorce is final and we're together, with the kids..."

"Stop the car. I want you to turn around and take me back home. We have nothing more to talk about."

"I won't, Nadine, until you listen to me." Trace twisted his hands on the steering wheel, his jaw clenched. "My marriage to Tina was a mistake..."

"Don't even start trying to explain away what

you have done. You made vows and promises. You broke them each time you went out with me, and I helped...." Nadine couldn't help the catch in her voice as she thought of the time they had spent together. "You made me an unwitting part of that, and I can't forgive you. Not now." She bit her lip, unable to articulate the anger and frustration that flowed through her. "I want you to turn around and bring me back home, Trace. Now."

He slowed down, and Nadine breathed a sigh of relief. But when he pulled in to a field and stopped, she became frightened. Trace turned the car off and turned slowly to her. Panic shot through her as she kept her eyes on him while fumbling for the door handle. "What are you doing?"

"You don't have to be afraid of me, Nadine." He shook his head, reaching out to touch her hair. "I'm not going to hurt you. I wouldn't do that to you."

Her fingers scrabbled at the handle. *Please open, please open,* she prayed. With a quick jerk she yanked on the handle. She jumped out of the car, stumbled as her coat fell out of the car and tangled around her legs. The interior light of the car shone feebly on the freshly plowed field. She tried to run, tripped on a lump of dirt and regained her balance.

Trace got out of the car, and she tried to increase her speed.

"Nadine, don't run. You'll hurt yourself," Trace warned.

She kept moving awkwardly, her feet unable to respond to her head. Hurry, hurry, she urged, her ankle twisting as she hit another furrow, unable to find even ground.

"I'm not coming after you, Nadine. Just stop." His voice came from farther away and she spared a glance over her shoulder.

The car was well behind her, and she could see Trace's figure silhouetted against the open door of the car.

"Come back, Nadine. I'll drive you home."

Still she hesitated. She was too far away from town to walk back, especially in the dark. But she had to get one thing straight before she would sit in the vehicle beside him. "What about your wife?"

"What about her?" he called back, his voice impatient. "We've been over that already. I'm getting a divorce. I told you it happened before I met you."

Nadine couldn't believe he could be so obtuse. "Doesn't matter," she replied, still facing him, the lights of the vehicle shining in her eyes. "I won't go out with you, Trace."

Suddenly he banged his fists on the roof of the car, startling Nadine. "You have to change your mind, you have to," he yelled. Nadine took another step back, ready to run again. Trace sounded out of control, and she was frightened.

"Trace, calm down. You don't know what you're saying," she replied. *Please, Lord, keep me safe. Send him away,* she prayed.

He jumped into the car and slammed the door shut. He started it up, threw it into Reverse and gunned the engine. Dirt flew as he backed out onto the road. Her prayer was about to be answered.

Nadine watched the glow of his taillights as they receded in the distance, the roar of his engine slowly growing fainter as the chill of the evening finally made itself known.

What had she done? What had she prayed for? He was gone and she was alone.

But even as the quickening breeze sucked warmth away from her, even as she looked around growing more and more confused and frightened, even with that, she had the conviction she had done the wiser thing. Trace was out of control, totally unreasonable.

Her eyes slowly became accustomed to the dark. A pale crescent moon hung in the sky above her, shedding a faint illumination on the land.

For now, all she could see was that she was walking in an open, plowed field. Across the road, another open field. To her left a row of trees marking the quarter line, and beyond that some more bush.

"Don't panic, and don't cry," she told herself as she carefully picked her way along. The furrows were deep and hard and the lack of light made it doubly difficult to walk. *Now what do I do, Lord?* she thought. *I know I did the right thing. I know I did. Please help me out of this.* She closed her eyes and continued her prayer for courage, strength and wisdom and anything else she might need to figure out how she was going to get back home.

She shivered in the chill wind and wished she had

her coat on. Then she remembered that it had fallen out of the car when she opened the door.

Nadine hurried as best as she could to the place the car had been parked, and in the thin light she saw a lump of material on the ground. "Thank you, Lord," she said, gratefully picking it up. Something heavy flew out of the pocket and clattered on the hard ground.

Her cell phone. "And thanks again," she prayed with gratitude. She picked it up and shrugged into her coat.

When she opened the phone the display showed three bars, indicating barely enough reception to make a call. And the Battery Low sign was on. "Okay, Lord. I guess it's just little miracles tonight."

She punched in the numbers to her house and lifted the phone, wincing as the static crackled in her ear. The phone at her home rang again and again. "Please answer it, Grandma, please," she pleaded. Finally she heard "Hello?"

Nadine sagged in relief. "Thank goodness you're still up, Grandma. It's Nadine."

"Nadine?…are you?" Crackling static broke into the conversation.

"I'm close to the lake." Nadine clutched the phone with one hand, her thin jacket with the other. The wind was picking up, and already her ears were getting cold. "Trace dropped me off somewhere in the country."

"Where?"

"I'm not sure." Nadine almost screamed the words, panicking as she looked around for any kind of landmark. "I'm at least half an hour's drive out of town."

"Which—" her words were drowned in a roar of static "—direction?"

"West. We drove west out of town, then he turned north." The static crackled louder. She turned back the way she had come to see if the reception got any better.

She was now walking into the chilly north wind. Her fingers were getting numb and her ears ached. But at least the static had died down.

"Is there anything that you recognize?"

Nadine hunched her shoulders against the wind and turned a slow circle, fear clutching her heart. Then she saw it. "I see a gas flare. I'm exactly east of it." Nadine relaxed somewhat. "Praise the Lord," she shouted. "I know where I am—up the Fraser road. Can you come and get me?"

"Yes. Of course. Just stay where you are." There was a moment's pause. "You are okay, aren't you?"

"Yes," Nadine replied, her voice unexpectedly shaky. "Yes, I am."

"Okay. I'll be…soon…" Grandma's voice faded away and Nadine lowered the now-dark handset. The battery was dead.

She flipped it closed, dropped it into her pocket and turned her back to the wind. Nadine wrapped her coat closer around her, tucking her hands into the wide sleeves. It was probably her least practical coat, a thin corduroy barn jacket she had picked up at a garage sale a few days ago because it was red.

Trace said she looked good in red. Trace, who was married.

Nadine sniffed, swallowed, determined not to cry. She felt cheap, humiliated and vulgar. She hadn't known he had a wife, children. He hadn't given her an inkling during their many conversations.

Nadine stopped walking, squeezing her eyes shut against the sting of tears. *Forgive me, Lord. I didn't know what was happening. I didn't know.*

Nadine looked up at the stars that spread away from her, feeling small, unimportant, disposable. She was walking along a dark, empty road, a tiny figure on a huge globe populated with many other tiny figures, each with their own sorrows and problems. What made her think her problems were so much worse than many others?

But then, even as she formed that thought, she knew that the same God who had created all of this from nothing also heard her prayers, whether softly whispered or shouted aloud.

And now, as she walked along the road, she prayed. As she prayed she felt God's peace wash over her, comfort her, strengthen and forgive her.

But her hands were still cold.

She shoved her hands farther up her sleeves and walked quickly, hoping the movement would get her blood flowing and warm her up. Behind her the bitter wind pushed itself through the thin material of her jacket, whipped her hair around her face and seeped into her bones.

Please, Lord, let Grandma's car start. Please let her drive quickly. I'm cold. Really cold. She shivered and pulled one hand out of her sleeve and pressed its meager warmth against one aching ear. After a while she traded and did it with the other. It helped a small amount, but her hands would not warm up.

Please, Lord. Let my grandmother come soon, before I can't move anymore.

She had walked for a little way when a faint light shone above a rise in the road ahead of her. It got brighter and brighter and then, finally, headlights blinded her as a vehicle topped the rise and roared toward her.

Not Grandma, she thought with a sinking heart. Grandma's little car had only one headlight and about half the horsepower. She paused, clutching her coat, waving her arm. She didn't care who it was, she was going to ask if they could at least drive her somewhere warm.

But the car drove past her, then slowed and turned around. Hallelujah, she thought, turning her head to watch the car as it pulled up beside her. Nadine frowned as it stopped and the driver's door opened. She couldn't stop herself from taking a step back as a tall figure straightened.

Clint Fletcher.

Nadine felt shock slam through her. How did he

know? What had made him come at precisely that moment?

Nadine hesitated, her heart beginning a staccato rhythm, her feet suddenly unresponsive. "How..."

"Doesn't matter." Clint moved around the car and opened the door for her. She took a few shaky steps, then got in, her heart racing. Clint slammed the door shut behind her and walked around the car, momentarily illuminated by the headlights. He got in on his side, closed his door and Nadine was surrounded by blissful warmth, blessed heat.

"Are you okay?" Clint asked, turning to her. He draped one arm over the steering wheel, while the other lay along the back of her seat.

She couldn't look at him, and only nodded. "My grandmother is coming...." She could hardly speak, her lips were so numb.

"Actually, she called me and asked me to come and get you."

The thrum of the engine and the gentle hum of the heater were the only sounds in the dark intimacy of the car. Nadine bit her lip, trying to stop her erratic breathing.

"Are you sure you're okay?" There was concern in his deep voice.

Nadine nodded, shivering as she began to warm up. She laid her head back, felt Clint's hand and sat up again. She swallowed, hardly knowing where to start. That Clint had come to get her, that he now sat beside her, concerned, caring, was more than she could comprehend.

His hand touched her head, curving around it, the warmth of his hand seeping through her hair making him very real.

"He didn't hurt you, did he?" Clint's fingers tightened their hold momentarily.

"No. No, he didn't."

"Good."

Silence again.

Clint shifted his weight, and then his hands engulfed hers, warming them. "You're freezing," he said quietly, rubbing her hands with vigor. "How long have you been out here?"

"About an hour, maybe more." She still couldn't look at him, still trying to absorb what had happened, what was happening now.

"Trace just drop you off?"

She shook her head. "I could have gotten a ride back to town with him, but I didn't think it was wise to stay around him anymore. He was quite…upset."

"Upset? Why?" Clint rubbed harder, then stopped when Nadine winced. "Sorry," he murmured, pressing her hands between his large warm ones.

"He—" Nadine's voice caught on that and then the words came tumbling out. "He's married, Clint. He has two kids and a wife, named Tina. They've been separated for a while. He wants to file for a divorce." Nadine turned to Clint, her fingers entangling with his. "I didn't know anything about it. I couldn't believe he would do that to her, to me.…" She bit her lip, holding back the tears. She had said she wasn't going to cry over Trace's duplicity, but it hurt.

Clint looked down, his thumbs caressing the backs of her hands.

"I broke up with him a few days ago, he came over tonight. He wanted me to come back," Nadine continued.

Clint raised his head at that, his eyes narrowed. "You broke up with him?"

Nadine nodded, feeling foolish. "It wasn't much of a relationship. I don't think I really cared much for him."

"Why not?"

Nadine could see the soft glow of his eyes, remembered the kiss he had given her, their conversation in the restaurant. He had come for her. Grandma had asked him to, but he still had come for her. She squeezed his hands as she took a deep breath and a chance. "I like someone else better."

Clint's thumbs slowed and he released her one hand, his coming up to lightly touch her cheek. "That's good," he said softly. Their eyes met in understanding and Nadine felt her breath slowly leaving her body. His fingers stilled and moved from her face to her neck.

"What are you doing?" she whispered inanely.

"Something I probably should have done years ago." He slid his fingers around her neck as his eyes held hers. Mesmerized, she drifted toward him. He drew her closer and then, finally, oh finally, their lips touched.

Hesitantly at first, as if the intimacy was too much to absorb at once. Then his hand tightened, pulled her nearer, and fitted his mouth closer, his other arm coming around to pull her against the solid warmth of his chest.

Nadine's eyes drifted shut, her hand slipped upward, across the breadth of his shoulder, around his neck. He was warm, solid, real.

She kissed him back, their lips moving carefully, exploring and discovering at the same time. This was where she should be. It was as if a mocking echo of her past had finally been stilled here, in Clint Fletcher's arms.

She drew slightly back, her fingertips lightly touching his cheek.

His features became serious then as his fingers carefully explored her face. "You're so beautiful," he whispered. "I can't believe you're here."

"I'm not beautiful," she said, her lifelong insecurity around this man making her unable to absorb the reality of Clint Fletcher touching her, kissing her, telling her these wonderful things.

He bent over and stopped her words with his mouth. "You are beautiful," he murmured against her lips. He kissed her again, making her insides melt with wonder. "I've always thought so."

She placed her hands against his shoulders, giving herself some room, barely able to take what he was giving her. "But you went out with Sabrina. You used to flirt with Leslie...."

Clint smiled a crooked smile and traced her lips

with his thumb. "Once a reporter..." He let the sentence hang as he shook his head. "Okay, if we get this stuff out of the way, can I kiss you again?"

Nadine laid her head against the headrest, her hands enfolded in his, as she tried to let her mind catch up to reality. "I guess so," she answered, her voice shaky.

He brushed a strand of hair away from her temple. "I always admired you, liked you, thought you were beautiful. But I was always a little afraid of your quick tongue and those penetrating brown eyes that look right into a man's dark, black soul."

Nadine frowned, her eyes traveling over his familiar features, his firm chin, his hazel eyes that now gazed intently at her. "I wasn't like that," she protested lamely.

"I didn't mind, even though at times I resented the way you made me look at myself and my life. I went out with your sister because she was easy to be with. At first it was attraction. But later, as I got to know you, I came as much to have an excuse to see you and talk to you." He drew her closer, laying her head against his shoulder. "I should have broken up with her sooner and I'm not proud of that part, but I liked your family so much. I liked coming over and talking to your father. I liked the way your family expressed their faith so easily, and I wanted a part of that." He paused a moment, his thumb making lazy circles against her temple. "My mom used to take me to church once in a while, but God's name was never spoken outside of that building.

Life just went on. Then I came here and started going out with Sabrina. I used to call, hoping you would answer and not Sabrina or Leslie, so I would have a chance to talk to you. You used to challenge me not only in my actions but in my faith. You made me realize that God was real and that we were accountable. You told me more than anyone ever did. Don't you remember what we used to talk about?''

Nadine closed her eyes, her cheek pressed against Clint's shirt, his warmth melding with hers. "I remember. I liked talking to you. I liked you. I could never figure out why Sabrina broke up with you."

Clint's thumb slowed and she felt his chest lift in a gentle sigh. "She didn't break up with me. I broke up with her."

Nadine stiffened in surprise, pulling away from him. "You did?"

"When I was in Europe, I knew I couldn't stay with her. Then when I became a Christian I knew I had to be with you. I found out about your father too late. I wanted to be there for you. Then I came back and you were engaged to Jack."

He spoke Jack's name with a soft contempt that made Nadine smile. She let his words wrap themselves around her, a balm to her wounded and lonely soul.

"I've always cared about you, Nadine." He pressed a kiss against her temple. "I found out too late that you broke up with Jack. Then your mother was so sick. So I left you alone. And when I took over from Uncle Dory…''

''My mother had just died and all I did was snap at you.''

''I think I was always a little afraid of you.'' He laughed. ''Even when I saw you walking down this road, all alone, knowing you must be freezing, I wanted nothing more than to stop the car, run out and grab you, and I didn't dare.''

Nadine smiled, trying to imagine the picture. ''Why?''

''It's your eyes, remember?'' Clint laid his chin on her head, rubbing it slowly over her hair.

Nadine could only close her eyes and let herself be wooed by a voice she had so often longed would say the things he said.

''A lot of people knew that I envied my sisters a bit,'' she said, her hand playing with a button on his coat. ''And they were right.'' She lifted her head and with a bemused expression touched his beloved features. ''But only because of you, Clint. Only because of you.''

He shook his head lightly. ''You never had to, Nadine.'' He bent over and once again their lips met, their souls joined.

Chapter Twelve

Nadine didn't want to move, nestled in Clint's embrace—a place she never thought she would end up when she left the apartment a few hours earlier. Clint reluctantly loosened his hold and though they parted, his hand still held on to hers.

"I should take you home," Clint said with a smile as he tenderly brushed a strand of hair back from her face. "Your grandmother will be worrying."

"No, she won't. The longer I'm gone, the happier she'll be."

"Why is that?" Clint looked puzzled.

Nadine tilted her head to one side, a bemused expression on her face. "My grandma, the eternal matchmaker, has been trying to get us together since you went out with Sabrina."

He quirked his mouth into a crooked smile and touched her lips lightly with his fingers, tracing them almost reverently. "She's a pretty smart lady."

"I'm sure she'll be thrilled when we get back to the apartment."

"Then we had better get back and make her life a little brighter." Clint let his fingers linger on her face, then reluctantly dropped his hand to start the car.

Nadine sat back and watched him as he put the car in gear, glanced idly over his shoulder and spun the wheel with one hand to pull onto the road.

He glanced sidelong and as their eyes met, it was like a caress. Clint reached over and caught her hand in his own. Then he returned his attention to the road, leaving Nadine free to study him with a boldness she never had before.

His nose didn't have the long narrowness generally associated with "handsome" men, his chin jutted out just a little, his lips were full, not thin and aristocratic. Taken all together they created a face that drew eyes back to him for a second look. And when he smiled, his aloof demeanor melted into a boyish appeal.

But even as Nadine analyzed his face, she knew that his features were only the surface, a way of identifying Clint apart from other men. Beneath his handsome face lay what drew her to him, a man of faith in God, integrity and strong values. A man of substance.

He must have sensed her scrutiny, because he glanced her way, two small furrows creasing his forehead just above his nose like two parentheses. "What's the matter?"

"Not a thing," she said quietly, covering the hand that held hers with her other. "I'm so thankful you came for me. It was an answer to prayer." She traced the back of his hand and impulsively raised it to her face. "Thanks again," she said softly, pressing a kiss against it. His fingers curled against her face and Nadine winged a silent prayer of thanks heavenward.

Nadine wondered what it was going to be like to go to work tomorrow, knowing he would be there, just down the hall.

Tonight she had seen a part of him that still seemed unreal. It fit with what she had seen at other times—the evening in the restaurant, the day he had come to the Foodgrains Project. She had read his article from that day and seen yet another facet to his nature. His reserve hid depths that she looked forward to exploring. He was dependable, steady and true.

Clint slowed as he came to town, as if reluctant to bring other people into what was so new between them. He clutched Nadine's hand a little harder. "First thing tomorrow morning I have to go to Calgary for a meeting, and then I'm supposed to fly to Toronto from there." He turned to her, his eyes mirroring the regret that Nadine suddenly felt. "I won't be in the office this week, but I hope to be back Thursday. Can I call you?"

Nadine nodded slowly, the very newness of their being together precluding anything else from her. She felt a keen disappointment that she dared not express. Not yet. She had no intention of letting things move as quickly as she had with Trace, yet she had so hoped to have an opportunity to cement the fragility of their beginnings.

She wondered what God was trying to teach her with this. It didn't seem fair.

"I wish I didn't have to go," he said, holding her hand. "I wish we could spend some ordinary time together."

"I know" was all she said.

They drove on in silence as Nadine clung to the memory of what had happened tonight, hoping it would hold her through the week until Thursday.

When Clint dropped her off he declined a cup of tea with an exultant grandma. What had happened between them was too new and unformed, so when he left, all he did was touch her hand surreptitiously and send her a wink as he stepped into his car.

"So what do I do with this?" Allison stood in front of Nadine's desk the next day, her hands holding the sheaf of notes she had taken the week before.

Nadine looked up at her, gathering her scattered thoughts.

"I'm supposed to get these into a coherent article by this afternoon?" Allison lifted her hand as if in surrender. "I thought you were going to write it up this weekend. I don't have the background on this company that you do."

"That's why I asked you to write it up." Nadine smiled absently at Allison as her intercom beeped.

"You've got a caller on line one." Sharlene's voice came in over the intercom.

"You'll do just fine, Allison," Nadine said, waving her away. "Now get to work. I'll vet it for you once you're done." She punched the button and picked up the phone, effectively dismissing her new reporter.

Allison looked down at the notes again and then left.

"Hello," Nadine said with a grin at Allison's expression as she left. Nadine tucked the phone under one ear, cleaning up the papers on the desk and replacing them in a folder.

"Miss Laidlaw?"

"Yes."

"I'm the lady who's going to meet you Thursday."

Nadine frowned, flipping over the pages of her desk calendar. Nothing was written down on Thursday. "Can I ask who is calling?"

"I'm the lady who wrote the letter."

Nadine clutched the handset, her heart fluttering as it all came back. How could she have forgotten?

"Five o'clock work out for you?" the harsh voice continued.

"Yes," Nadine assured her, pulling a pen and a pad toward her. "I'll be there. How will I know you?"

"Like I said, I'll be wearing a green sweatshirt and gray pants. I know what you look like. Just stay in the main gymnasium and I'll find you."

"Okay. Five o'clock, main gym. Gotcha."

"No one else will know or be there?"

Nadine hesitated, wondering if she was getting set up. The lady sounded like a bit of a kook, but she didn't dare offend her. She had waited too long to find out what this informer knew. "No one else will know."

"Good. I'll see you there." And with that her mystery caller hung up.

Nadine laid the phone carefully in the cradle and, blowing out her breath, leaned back. There was altogether too much mystery surrounding this woman, and for a moment Nadine was tempted to let it all go.

But she knew she couldn't. She had gladly passed off the accident article to Allison, but this she had to follow up on.

The day slipped by. Phone calls took more time than they should and it was late afternoon before Nadine had a chance to go over the layout once more with the typesetter, double-check the articles for errors. Their ad accounts were up, thanks to a hardworking sales staff. Nadine could justify taking a two-page spread for the Foodgrains Harvest.

She had already selected which pictures they were going to scan in and how much space they were going to take up on the page. Now it was a matter of going over Clint's article one last time.

Clint's style was straightforward. He hadn't written many articles since he'd come here, but his professionalism showed in this one.

Clint wasn't a passionate writer, but a deep conviction showed in how he presented the project. He had distilled an entire afternoon of interviews and observation into a thoughtful treatment of giving and sharing. In a diplomatic style he pointed out a responsibility to share wealth with those less fortunate, but to realize that as the sharing was done, the giver was only passing on what had been entrusted by God. It was written as a news article, but it had glimpses of challenge to the reader.

Nadine felt a deep satisfaction well up in her as she read Clint's story. It had depth, it had a personal touch and it left the reader thinking. He presented his story in a way that made people stop and reassess their own lives and blessings.

She laid down the paper, her chin in her hand as she stared into space.

Was it possible that this articulate and careful man was the same person who had held her in his arms last night, had kissed her? She sighed as she thought of the days ahead, the office suddenly emptier with him gone, a space in her own life that had never been there before.

She often had to remind herself that he had come for her, that he had held her, kissed her. Without much effort she recalled their conversation in the inn. Their relationship had changed, had moved to a level she had dreamed of, but never dared see as reality.

She was seized with a loneliness that was even

harsher and deeper than before.

She missed him.

Clint waited while Sharlene patched him into Nadine's office, feeling a moment's apprehension. He felt as nervous as a teenager and had to remind himself that he was Nadine's boss as well as...

He wasn't sure what, exactly. He only knew that he had no intention of letting Nadine slip out of his hands again.

"Hello." Nadine's hesitant voice made him smile.

"Hi, this is your boss. I was wondering if you have some important school-board meeting to cover on Thursday night."

"Wally's doing that." She sounded reserved.

"No volleyball games?"

"I've got Allison on them."

Clint leaned his forehead against the cool window of his motel room. He wished he was back in Derwin, back in his office just down from Nadine's. He wanted to hold her, remind himself that she had come willingly into his arms. He didn't know where to begin with this girl who had had him tied up in knots for so many years. "Then you can spare some time for me?"

"Thursday night? This Thursday night? What time?"

"I thought I could pick you up at about six from your apartment."

She was silent a moment, then said almost breathlessly, "I'll be meeting Allison at the gym before that, but that sounds okay."

"Okay, then. I'll call you once more, just to confirm." Goodness, he thought, sounds as if you're making hotel reservations.

And as he said his final farewells, sounding distinctly unloverlike, he thought that was what it had felt like.

He wished he could go back to Derwin right now, before Nadine changed her mind about him.

By Thursday afternoon Nadine was in such a dither, she couldn't concentrate on her work. She didn't know what to attribute which emotion to. Clint was taking her out that night and maybe they could start again. In a few hours she would, hopefully, find out the truth about her father. And after that...

She had committed herself to meeting this lady, yet she felt that she was betraying Clint.

You're not going to do anything with it! she reminded herself. It's just for information.

She tried to keep herself busy and her eyes off the clock, but it didn't work. Finally at about four-thirty she gave up. She didn't have to feel guilty about not working until five. Goodness knows she had spent enough overtime hours at the office.

She drove home, then showered and changed, her mind going back and forth between a loyalty to Clint, who wanted her to leave Skyline alone, and a need to find out what this lady knew.

Thankfully Grandma was gone, which meant she didn't need to explain her actions. She hadn't told Grandma about the mystery lady, just in case it turned out to be a hoax. Nadine didn't want to disappoint her.

A number of teams were warming up by the time Nadine entered the foyer, the shrill sounds of whistles echoing through the gym. She stood in the doorway of one of the gyms, but didn't spot a green sweatshirt. She wandered restlessly around the hallways, returning every few minutes to check.

Half an hour later Nadine's stomach was in knots. It was 5:20. Clint hadn't phoned before she left the office, so she assumed he would come to the house at six as they originally had planned. She tried to phone her grandmother, but there was no answer. From 5:15 on she had stayed in the main gym, thankful that no game was being played there. Allison was shooting pictures in the other gym.

At five-thirty she was pacing the hallway. She had maybe fifteen more minutes before she absolutely had to leave.

What if this was all a hoax? she wondered as she glanced at her watch. What if Skyline had deliberately planted this lady, was doing this just to sabotage her life?

Don't be ridiculous, she chided herself. You're getting paranoid because you're feeling guilty.

She was wondering if she should leave a note. Where? How? "Dear lady in the green sweatshirt and gray pants, I had to leave for an important date"? A date she'd been waiting for all her life.

Nadine almost laughed aloud. It was as if she had to choose between silencing the echoes of the past or grasping a hope for the future.

Nadine shook her head, glancing once more at her watch. Her stomach tightened as the hands moved steadily on to six o'clock.

Was she sabotaging a chance with Clint all for nothing? But no, she reminded herself. He had originally said six o'clock. Hopefully he would wait a little while.

She stepped back into the gym. She would make one more circle and then leave.

Right away Nadine saw a green sweatshirt. And gray pants. Her shoulders sagging in relief, she ran around the edge of the court and caught up to the slight female figure.

"Excuse me," Nadine said, tapping her on the shoulder. "Were you looking for me? Nadine Laidlaw."

The woman turned around. Slight, fair-haired, streaks of gray glinting at her temples. Her eyes seemed weary, her smile forced as she looked up at Nadine. "I thought that was you." She shoved her hands into the kangaroo pocket of her hooded sweatshirt and indicated with her head that she wanted to talk outside.

Nadine followed her, trying to get her pounding heart to slow down. She's just going to answer a few questions, nothing major, she thought. Don't expect too much. But Nadine had to wipe her sweaty palms off on her pants as they stepped out of the noisy foyer into the relative quiet of outside.

The woman lit a cigarette and Nadine was surprised to see the flame of the match tremble. She pulled in a deep drag, blew it out and then looked at Nadine. "My name is Chantelle Hayward. My brother, Gordon, used to work for Skyline. He worked with your father."

This was it, Nadine thought. What we've been waiting for all this time. *Thank you, Lord. Thank you.*

"My brother was hired by Skyline almost seven years ago, just a month before your father died." Chantelle left the cigarette in her mouth as she dug into the pocket of her jeans. She pulled out an envelope and handed it to Nadine. "Six months ago he tried to commit suicide and failed. Before he tried he wrote a suicide note."

Nadine glanced at Chantelle's face and then back at the envelope.

"Go on," urged Chantelle, shoving the envelope into Nadine's hands. "Take it. It's just a photocopy. I read it already. Know what it says. He worked for that company for two months after the accident and he hadn't been the same since. I wanted to know what caused it." She laughed. It was a bitter sound. "I almost wish I hadn't."

"What happened?" Nadine asked, her voice breaking. "That he tried to commit suicide, I mean."

Chantelle shrugged. "Gordon wasn't what you'd call scholarship material, so we were really glad when he got this job." She took another drag from her cigarette. "But he was there when your father died and he hasn't been able to forget it. He'd been threatened by unknown people to keep his mouth shut. But I knew you wrote articles about them and you're not afraid to call them what they are. Cheats." Chantelle waved the burning cigarette at the letter, the smoke wreathing between them. "Your father didn't die because he was careless. He died because of my brother, but mostly because of Skyline." Chantelle dropped her cigarette and ground it out with the toe of her running shoe. "The letter explains everything." She looked up at Nadine, her eyes almost glowing in the gathering dusk.

Nadine held up the envelope and looked at it once again. "I'll read it. For sure I'll read it. Thanks." She was fully aware of the passing time, and now that she had fulfilled one obligation, she was anxious to get home.

"I want to see those guys pulled down for what they did to Gordon, to your family." Chantelle took a step forward, her eyes burning with intensity. For a moment Nadine felt afraid of what she saw in Chantelle Hayward's eyes. "You can show everyone what they are. Now you have proof."

Nadine swallowed. "I'll do what I can, Chantelle."

Chantelle stared hard at her. "I hate them, Laidlaw. I really hate them." She pulled out her cigarette package and withdrew another cigarette. "I hate what they do to the community, I hate what they did to my family. They're a pack of lying, cheating..."

Nadine frowned as she listened to Chantelle rant, her anger gathering momentum.

Nadine thought of her own anger, her own sorrow. Yes, she wanted to see justice done. Yes, she wanted to see Skyline brought down just as Chantelle Hayward did. But surely, Nadine thought, she didn't have the same deep, intense hatred that Chantelle did?

"So what are you going to do?" Chantelle asked, finishing another cigarette.

Nadine pocketed the letter. "First I'm going to read the letter and find out exactly what your brother knew. I'll take it from there."

"You're not going to wuss out on me, now, are you?" Chantelle glared at her. "It's all in there. In that letter. You read it." Chantelle walked backward toward the gym, still talking. "I'll call you in a couple of days and you can tell me then." She pulled open the door, a flood of noise spilling out.

"I will." The door slammed shut, cutting off the sounds of the tournament inside. Nadine leaned back against the wall, her insides trembling in reaction and a touch of fear. Chantelle had seemed almost fanatical, and Nadine wondered what in the world was in the letter.

She glanced at her watch. Six-fifteen! She turned and began running. It would take her ten minutes to get home. The thought that Clint might be waiting hurried her steps and lightened her heart. A date. A real date with Clint.

Her feet pounded out a steady rhythm as her breathing became more labored. Only a little farther, she reassured herself. Just a few more blocks. *Just let him be there, Lord. Let him be waiting.* She didn't dare stop, could hardly keep going and almost skidded around the corner to her street. When she saw only her grandmother's car and her old car in front of the house, she slowed her pace, clutching her side, her chest heaving.

By the time she got to the apartment, her breathing was slowing but her legs were trembling with a combination of the extra exertion and anticipation. She walked into the entrance, her heart still pounding.

"Hey, Grandma," she called out, kicking off her shoes and setting them neatly in the porch. "I'm home."

"Nadine." Grandma's voice chided her from the end of the hallway just as Nadine hung up her coat. "Where have you been?"

Nadine stepped into the kitchen, her heartbeat finally slowing. "I had to meet someone for an interview at the school."

Grandma stood in the kitchen, her arms folded across her chest, her head tilted to one side. "Clint has been here waiting for you. He just left."

Nadine's heart stopped, beat once, then began racing again, this time in fear. "What—what did you say?"

"Clint just left."

"But I tried to phone you."

Danielle Laidlaw looked sheepish. "I wanted to have a nap, so I turned off the ringer. I remembered at six to turn it back on."

Nadine took a slow breath, willing her heart to still. "How long was he waiting here?"

"He came here at a quarter past five. Then someone named Allison phoned here at a quarter past six asking for you. I asked if she wanted to talk to Clint. She did and then he left." Grandma walked over to Nadine. "What is happening? Were you and Clint supposed to have a date tonight, and who is this Allison?"

"She's a new reporter at the *Times*." Nadine chewed her lip, remembering how she had told Clint that she was to meet Allison at the gym. Now it looked for sure as if she was hiding something. What should she do now? "Did Clint say where he was going?"

"He just thanked me for the tea and then left."

"I gotta go, Grandma." She turned and ran into the entrance. "I don't know when I'll be back. Don't wait up for me." As she grabbed her car keys off the hook, she flashed a nervous smile at her hovering grandmother. "I'll tell you all about it later."

Her stomach was churning by the time she pulled in to a parking spot. It would have been just as fast to run back from her house, but the stitch in her side gave lie to that thought.

As she strode down the sidewalk, she glanced at

the vehicles. No sign of Clint's red car. She took a
shortcut across the lawn and just as she came to the
corner of the gym, she heard a vehicle drive out of
the parking lot.

With a sinking heart she watched Clint Fletcher's
vehicle slow and then spin around the corner and
down the road.

Chapter Thirteen

Nadine leaned against the brick wall of the gym as she watched Clint's car leave. Only then did the enormity of what she had done hit her.

"You still here? I thought you were gone."

Nadine felt her heart stop at Chantelle's all-too-familiar voice. She turned. "I was, but I was hoping to meet someone."

"That new guy at the paper?" Chantelle rubbed one hand along the side of her pants. "You just missed him."

A coldness gripped Nadine's chest. "How do you know?"

Chantelle snapped her gum. "Talked to him. Told him some of what I told you. Figured it wouldn't hurt if two people knew the story."

Her hands felt like ice, her heart a heavy weight. Clint knew why she had come here, why she had missed him.

"He didn't seem real interested at first," warned Chantelle. "But when I told him that it was about Skyline he looked as mad as I felt."

Each word she spoke added to the heaviness in her chest. Nadine nodded quickly in acknowledgment, then turned, ran to her car and jumped in. Her head ached and her side still hurt by the time she pulled up in her driveway. But no sporty red car stood parked in front of the house.

Nadine laid her head against the steering wheel and allowed herself a few moments of tears. Was the letter worth it? She didn't know what was in it, but even if it proved that her father was completely innocent, would it change anything? She would probably not write the article. But would Clint know that?

Nadine remembered again Chantelle's bitterness and knew that once she herself had had the same burning need for revenge. But it wasn't solely up to her to bring justice into the world. She had done what she could and she now had to learn to let go. Justice belonged in God's hands, not her puny ones.

But Clint.

Her stomach plunged again as she thought of him sitting here at her house, waiting for her.

Can we back up and do this again, Lord? she prayed. *I'd like another try. I'll make the right choice this time.* But as she looked up, the lights of her apartment extra bright through her tears, she knew she'd had her chance and had made her choices. The letter in her pocket wasn't worth the opportunity she had thrown away with Clint Fletcher.

She bit her lip and indulged in a few more minutes of tears. Then, palming away the moisture from her cheeks, she opened the door and trudged back to the apartment.

Nadine slipped into the apartment and, with a tired sigh, kicked off her shoes for the second time in fifteen minutes.

"Is that you, Nadine?" called her grandmother from the living room.

"Yes," she called out, suddenly bone weary. She wanted to go to her bedroom, shove her head under a pillow and stay there until the spirit moved her to leave. Which, in her present state of mind, might be never.

"Come sit with me a minute and tell me what is going on."

Nadine stopped at the doorway to the living room. "Nothing is going on, Grandma. I missed Clint. I didn't know when he was coming, that's all."

Danielle turned to her granddaughter, her mouth drawn tight. "You leave the poor man sitting here for an hour and you say 'That's all'?"

"What else am I supposed to say?" grumped Nadine. She didn't need her grandmother's censure right now—she had enough self-disgust to spare. "I don't want to talk about it, Grandma."

"Well, I do. Clint Fletcher is a fine young man. He's handsome, smart and a sincere Christian. Quite a potent combination, I'd say."

I'd say, too, thought Nadine as she dropped into a nearby chair.

"Where were you, Nadine?"

"In the first place, I didn't know what time Clint was coming," she answered, ignoring her grandmother's question.

"He said he phoned the office. Where were you?" Danielle repeated.

In answer, Nadine slid her hand into her pocket and pulled out the envelope Chantelle had given her. "I went to meet with a lady who had some more information on how Dad died."

Danielle had opened her mouth to shoot another question at Nadine, but obediently closed it at what her granddaughter said.

Nadine waved the envelope back and forth, staring at it, wondering what it said and yet, somehow, not caring. It couldn't begin to make up for what she had passed up. Would she be able to explain? How would it sound? *"You asked me to lay off Skyline and then I keep you waiting while I go digging for more information to use against them"?*

"Is the information in the envelope?"

Nadine nodded, suddenly bone weary and exhausted.

"Aren't you going to read it?"

Nadine sat up, holding the envelope between her fingers. "I guess I may as well. Just so that standing Clint up wasn't all for nothing." She ripped open one end and pulled out the photocopy Chantelle had given her. Pursing her lips, she unfolded it and turned it over to read the tight, crabbed writing.

It felt eerie reading what was supposed to have been read only after the writer had taken his own life. She skimmed over the references to personal events, events that would matter only to Chantelle. And then, halfway down, there it was. Her father's name. Nadine slowed her reading. As if to help, she traced the words slowly with her finger, her heart pounding with the words she read, her hands suddenly clammy.

"What does it say, Naddy? You look stunned."

Nadine finished reading, staring at the letter. Then she slouched back in the easy chair, dropping her head against the back of it. "It wasn't Dad's fault, Grandma," she whispered, letting the letter drop into her lap. "It wasn't his fault. Just like we figured. That poor boy."

Danielle got up and pulled the piece of paper easily out of Nadine's limp hands. She held the letter at arm's length, squinting irritably at it. She put on the reading glasses hanging around her neck. Her mouth moved slowly as she read the words, and when she was finished, she looked at Nadine.

"Who is this from?"

Nadine blew her breath out, her bangs fluffing up as she did so. "Believe it or not, it's a suicide note from a young man who worked with Dad the day he died."

"Suicide?" Grandma pressed one hand to her

chest, the other reaching out blindly for some support. Nadine jumped to her feet and caught her arm.

"It's okay, Grandma. He didn't kill himself. And this is just a photocopy." Still holding the letter, Nadine led her back to the couch. She helped her grandmother sit down and then smoothed out the now-crumpled piece of paper. She glanced over it once more, rereading what he had said about her father's death.

Gordon Hayward had been training as a faller. He had been sent out into the bush totally green. He had made a mess of the trees, and a few days later Jake Laidlaw had come in to help. Jake had told him to wait in the truck where it was safe while he cleaned up. Then a Skyline foreman had come by and sent Gordon, over his protests, back to falling. Gordon had gotten too close to Jake, and a tree he was cutting went the wrong way and killed Jake. When the foreman came by again to check on Gordon he found him crouched in front of the pickup, crying. The foreman told Gordon that he was liable and could end up paying a fine. The Haywards were counting on his paycheck, and other jobs were scarce, so Gordon signed a written statement made out by Skyline saying that he'd heard the foreman warn Jake about his work.

Gordon worked for them until he found another job. But Jake's dying cries haunted him. The knowledge that he had implicated and killed an innocent man stayed with him and he couldn't bear the burden any longer.

"How did you get it?"

Grandma's quiet question jolted Nadine back to the present. She pulled her scattered thoughts together. "His sister Chantelle. I met her at the gym tonight." Nadine folded up the letter and laid it on the coffee table in front of the couch. "I got a letter from her a while ago, telling me that she had something I should see. We finally connected a few days ago and had made arrangements to meet tonight at the gym."

"I wish I could say I was glad," whispered Danielle, her fingers resting on her lips. "But to think of Jake lying there…" Her words were choked off and she began to cry.

Nadine pulled her close, hugging her fiercely, her own emotions unstable.

Six years of speculation, finally answered. Her father, killed by the carelessness of an inexperienced logger, covered up by an irresponsible company. Nadine clenched her teeth when she thought of what Gordon had said about listening to the dying cries of her father.

Danielle straightened and brushed her tears off her wrinkled cheeks. She turned to Nadine and touched her cheek lovingly, her eyes still bright with tears. "I'm sorry you had to be the one to find this out, Nadine. You've worked so hard on this, done so much."

Nadine shook her head. "I didn't do anything. Nothing has changed. Dad is still dead."

"Yes, but it is comforting to know that he wasn't

at fault.'' Danielle sniffed and then got up to get some tissues.

Nadine slouched back against the couch, her hands clasped over her stomach. Her mind drifted back over the years. She easily imagined her father sitting in his leather recliner across their living room in their old house, a wreath of aromatic pipe smoke surrounding his head as he worked his way through the *Derwin Times*. Her mother would be bustling in the kitchen, putting the final touches on the meal, and she and her sisters would be sprawled over furniture and floor, books spread around them as they pretended to do homework. Home was a comfortable haven then. What would have happened if he still lived?

''I have to write something up on this.'' Nadine snatched the letter off the table and strode past her grandmother. She had to do something, anything, instead of dwelling on might-have-beens. She hadn't intended to write a story, but now she realized she had nothing to lose that she hadn't already lost.

She switched on her computer, riffled through her computer diskettes until she found one labeled Skyline. Once the computer was booted up, she popped it into the drive, opened up a new file and began typing.

An hour later she looked up from the screen and rubbed her neck, now tight with tension. She saved the article on a disk and, just to be on the safe side, E-mailed it to the office, as well.

She leaned back in her chair, her eyes closed,

wondering how she was going to work the article
into the paper. Editorial? Tie-in with the accident of
last week?

Why do it at all?

Nadine dragged her hands over her face and
sighed deeply. Why do it at all? She leaned over
and clicked the mouse on the Print command. She
needed to see it printed out, needed to hold it in her
hand.

She read the pages as they came out of the printer,
the editor in her pleased with what she had written.
The article had bite, punch and flowed smoothly. It
was the culmination of all the articles and editorials
she had ever done on Skyline.

Nadine lowered the papers with a sigh. She had
a wonderful article written with emotion and good
cause. After six years her own instincts about her
father's death had been proven correct. Tonight all
the questions had been answered, all the *i*'s dotted.

But as she thought of Clint, she knew the price
had been too great. Her heart felt like a square lump
in her chest as she looked at her article once again.

It gave her no satisfaction.

What have I done, Lord, she prayed, dropping it
on her desk and falling into her chair. *I gave up
something precious just to prove myself right.* She
spun her chair back and forth, back and forth, re-
criminations filling her head, fighting with memories
of Clint smiling at her across a table, holding her,
comforting her. All she had wanted as a young girl
had been given to her as a gift, and she had just
thrown it all away.

Chapter Fourteen

Clint wearily rubbed his eyes. This Thursday had been one of the longer days of his life. He had come directly to the office from the school, preferring to work rather than think about what had just happened tonight.

With a sigh he picked up the letter he'd received that morning from the newspaper's lawyer. Skyline hadn't filed anything yet, but their lawyers were still threatening.

He didn't know whether to ignore the threat or worry about it. The accountant's report and the lawyer's letter dealt with different aspects of the business, but they both said the same thing. A prolonged battle with Skyline would put the newspaper so far into the red that Clint stood to lose everything.

Clint dropped his head against the back of the chair, thinking of how quickly the evening had changed. He had left his meeting with high hopes and an eager expectation of seeing Nadine, of spending time with her. That she was gone when he came had been disappointing. But what that belligerent woman he'd met at the gym had told him had made everything turn completely around.

From the sound of the E-mail he'd just seen on the computer, Nadine was bound and determined to bring Skyline to justice, regardless of his wishes and needs. He thought he had laid out the consequences for the newspaper, thought he had given her enough reason to back off. But obviously it wasn't enough.

Did you think she was so terribly in love with you that she would give up a six-year battle just because you asked her to?

What could he possibly think he meant to her after spending a few evenings together? Nadine had made it quite clear what she thought of him, from the first time he stepped into this office.

Surely he hadn't imagined the way she'd looked at him when they'd shared a meal, the way she'd seemed to drift back against him when he came to her office? Too vividly he remembered how she had willingly gone into his arms that evening in the car. Surely her reaction was more than gratitude?

The timing of this week's meetings was terrible. How badly he had wanted to stay Monday and reinforce the fragile bond begun the evening before. He and Nadine had had no chance to solidify their relationship, if indeed they had one.

Clint got up and pulled his tie off, threw it into a corner and rolled up the sleeves of his shirt. Hands in his pockets, he walked to the window, staring past his blurred reflection to the meager light of the streetlights. Was it only a few months ago he had stood here with a sense of eager expectation, a realization that his life had come if not full circle, then at least to a point that he knew he should be? It was as if God had been slowly pushing him here by cutting off some opportunities and opening others. His job at the city newspaper had changed, become unsatisfying. Uncle Dory, out of the blue, had offered him his share of the business.

He had found out that Nadine was still single.

Clint leaned his forehead against the glass, the coolness soothing his tired head.

For a few days he'd thought his life was coming together, that it was finally getting some kind of cohesion. He had a business he loved and the affection of a woman who had been on his mind for years, a woman who was a Christian, a soul mate. It was as if all the things he had been seeking were there in one neat package.

And now it looked as if he was going to lose it all.

The refrain of a song drifted through his head. "All to Jesus I surrender, all to Him I freely give..."

Clint rolled his forehead against the glass. Too simplistic, he thought.

Surely it wasn't wrong to want to run a healthy business, to take care of it, to take all necessary steps to make sure that his employees had a job? He had tried to keep the newspaper in perspective, to keep a balance with his faith and his work.

Could Nadine say the same thing?

He straightened, shoving his hand through his hair. Easy for him to judge her. He still had his father. He and Clint didn't speak often with each other and had never been really close, so Clint didn't know how he would have reacted had his own father died under questionable circumstances.

But revenge? If that indeed was what Nadine wanted?

Clint shook his head and rubbed the back of his neck. He didn't want to judge Nadine. He wanted to love her. He wanted to take care of her. He wanted to show her that love and he didn't know how to do it.

Yes, you do.

Clint paused, the voice pulling him up short. It had come from his own thoughts, his own conscience. On a hunch, he walked over to his briefcase and, hunkering down, opened it. He hadn't unpacked it after his meeting and had taken it into the office after his aborted date with Nadine tonight.

In one corner of it lay his Bible. Clint took it out, closed the briefcase and straightened.

Still standing, he thumbed through the New Testament until he came to Corinthians. Then, with one hand in the pocket of his suit pants, the other holding the Bible as it lay open, he began to read the words that had struck him so many years ago.

"Love is patient, love is kind, it does not envy,

it does not boast, it is not proud. It is not rude, it is not self-seeking...." Clint paused at that one. Was it self-seeking to want to see his newspaper post a profit? His lawyer had consistently warned him against a battle with Skyline because of the cost, not because of the right or wrong of it.

Clint continued reading. "Love does not delight in evil, but rejoices with the truth. It always protects, always trusts, always hopes, always perseveres. Love never fails...."

Clint read on and then closed the book with a soft sigh. He ran his thumb over the worn edges of the pages, riffling them as what he had just read settled into his mind, finding the right places, a solution that would neatly fit.

And as he thought, Clint realized that in order for anything to fit, he would have to let go of some of the things he held too tightly. He would have to trust. It seemed too easy and it seemed too hard at the same time. Maybe it was a test, and if he passed, he would get whatever he wanted.

Clint laughed lightly at his own thoughts, at the idea of a small person like himself trying to find a way to entice God into giving him what he wanted, provided he played the game right. He laid his Bible on his desk, slowly sat down and closed his eyes in prayer.

Nadine sighed and rolled over. Six o'clock in the morning. The sun was barely up and she was wide-awake. Had been since five o'clock. And since five she had tried to find a way out of going to the office. It would be so much easier to stay home, avoid Clint, everything.

Again and again she relived the evening, imagining different scenarios—cutting Chantelle Hayward off, coming home on time and sharing the letter with Clint. Or not showing up at the gym at all and spending a delightful evening with Clint.

Finally she threw the blankets back in frustration and stalked to the bathroom. She didn't care if she woke Grandma up. She had to do something instead of lying in bed castigating herself for being so shortsighted.

Her anger at herself simmered through her shower, as she got dressed. She took extra care, pulling out an outfit that Sabrina and Leslie had chivied her into buying last spring. Narrow gray corduroy pants, snug T-shirt also in gray topped with a collarless tunic in an unusual shade of apricot that complemented her brown hair.

Nadine finished toweling off her hair and blew it dry, deciding to let it hang loose.

The way Clint liked it.

The kitchen was still dark when she tiptoed into it. She pulled out an apple, poured herself a glass of milk and ate her breakfast leaning against the counter behind her. Nadine was thankful that Grandma still slept. The last thing she wanted right now was a postmortem on what had happened last night. Bad enough that she would be seeing Clint in a few hours.

She drove to the office, and as she parked her car in her stall in the back of the building, she noticed with a thump of her heart that Clint was at the office already. With a feeling of apprehension, she unlocked the back door and walked down the darkened hallway past the cubicles of the copy editors. One of the computers was on in a cubicle, the screen saver bouncing around on the screen. Frowning, Nadine walked over to it and hit one of the keys. The E-mail program was on, and Nadine saw that the article she had written last night was on the screen.

Clint must have turned it on, she thought, her heart sinking. She had forgotten she had sent it as a backup.

She looked around, wondering where Clint was now. Then she walked past the darkroom and down the hallway to her office.

Pausing at the door, she glanced up the hallway to the front entrance and Clint's office. His door was open, but the room was dark. Puzzled, Nadine took a few steps closer.

A figure was slouched over the desk, one arm flung out.

In the early-morning light filtering in through the window she could see it was Clint. His head moved slightly, disturbing the papers underneath him.

He was sleeping.

Clint shifted and Nadine turned to leave, but he only sighed and settled again. Feeling like an intruder, she stepped into the office, closer to his desk. She watched him a moment, his hair falling across his forehead, his soft lips slightly parted. His firm jaw was stubbled, the collar of his shirt open. His one arm was flung across the desk, his other hung down, inches away from her. He looked vulnerable and utterly appealing. Nadine felt a gentle ache in her heart as she thought of all that she could have had and then, without thinking, reached over and carefully brushed his hair away from his forehead, her hand lingering on his cheek.

She didn't expect his eyes to open, and she froze as the hand that hung down reached up and caught hers.

"Hey, Nadine," he murmured as he blinked and slowly sat up, still holding her hand. He smiled blearily. "Come here," he said, his voice husky from sleep as he rose from his seat and tugged her toward him.

Surprise and shock threw her off balance and he easily pulled her into his embrace. His arms came around her, his chin rested on her head and she felt his chest rise and fall in a protracted sigh. She couldn't relax, knowing she needed to leave, not wanting to.

"Don't say anything," he murmured, holding her close, rubbing his stubbled chin on her hair. "I like this dream better."

You have to go, Nadine told herself, cherishing the feel of his arms around her, being surrounded by the warmth of him. You can't stay here, this isn't right, she thought. But she closed her eyes, allowing herself this one moment of wish fulfillment, this brief taste of might-have-beens. She let her hand slip around his neck, allowed her fingers to lightly touch his hair as she finally relaxed in his embrace. She felt so secure, so accepted, so cherished simply being herself.

She loved him.

The words began as a small thought but then, as she closed her eyes, they grew until they were so close to her lips, she had to say them. "I love you," she whispered in a voice so soft she wasn't even sure she had spoken them aloud.

She swallowed the lump in her throat and then, turning her head away from him, slipped out of his embrace and stood in front of him.

But his hand still held hers. Puzzled, she turned, only to see him staring at her with perfectly focused eyes, no sign of sleep clouding their piercing gaze.

Unnerved, she pulled on her hand again, but Clint held fast.

"What's happening, Nadine?" he asked.

She could only stare at him, aware of what she had just done. "I'm sorry," she whispered finally.

"For what?"

His quiet question hung, echoing lightly in the silence of the office.

"Everything," she said softly, looking down at their intertwined hands, unable to pull her hand free and unwilling to as she realized he had been fully awake when he'd held her so close a few moments ago. "Standing you up last night, not being honest with you..." She stopped, unable to say more.

His hand lifted her chin, cupping it. His eyes met hers, his mouth curved up in a half smile. "You've done nothing to be sorry for." He stepped closer, then, without any warning, he bent down and touched his lips to hers.

Nadine felt herself sway toward him, and her hand came up and rested against his wrinkled shirt, as if to support herself. Then his arms were around her again, his mouth on hers.

It made no sense.

It made perfect sense.

Nadine let herself slip away to a place she had never imagined would be hers again to discover. A place where mind, heart and spirit were one with another, a place of surrender and strength, of peace and tumult; Clint's arms surrounding her, his body warming hers, his mouth caressing hers. She returned his kisses, clung to him, exulted in his strength.

But when he reluctantly pulled away, tucking her head once again under his chin, she did not dare think what it could all mean.

They were silent, as if each needed to absorb what had once again happened between them, as if each was afraid to voice what might change what had just happened.

Nadine suddenly pulled away, looking up at him. "I know you saw what I wrote last night. I'm not going to run the article."

Clint frowned, as if puzzled by what she said.

"I just wrote it after I got the letter from Chantelle.'' Nadine looked down, fingering the cuff of her tunic top. ''I was upset. I had just found out the truth about my father. All those questions we've had about him were finally answered.'' She looked up at Clint, praying he would understand. ''I found out how he died, what happened....'' A wave of sorrow welled up as she remembered what Gordon had said about her father's cries. Her words were choked off and once again she was in Clint's arms. Hot tears slid past her eyelids and flowed down her cheeks.

''It's okay, Nadine. It's okay to cry,'' he murmured as he held her.

Nadine nodded. She drew in a steadying breath as the tears subsided. ''I'm sorry. It seems all I do lately around you is cry,'' she said with a shaky laugh.

''I don't mind,'' he said softly, his hand on her shoulder. He angled his head, his hand squeezing her shoulder. ''I want you to know, Nadine, that I think you should run the article on your father.''

Nadine frowned at him, surprised. ''What are you talking about? I thought Skyline was threatening the paper with a lawsuit?''

''So far it's just threats.'' Clint traced the track of a tear down Nadine's cheek, his eyes following the path of his finger. ''I would be lying if I said I wasn't concerned about it. But your battle with Skyline has shown me something important. The reason I went into this business to start with. To print the truth. To expose wickedness and collusion.'' He smiled a wry smile, absently stroking her hair away from her face, tucking it behind her ear. "I learned something from you in all of this. You have shown me how a child should love their parent and how strong love can be. I never cared for my parents that way."

"Please," she begged, shaking her head. "Don't look to me as an example of filial love. My mother and I had a totally different relationship."

"Probably, but you did the same for her that you did for your father. You sacrificed much for her. A career, a marriage—"

"Breaking my engagement to Jack wasn't a huge sacrifice," she interrupted.

"That's good to hear." He fiddled with a strand of her hair, sending delicate shivers down her spine at his casual touch. "You have always been someone who holds fast to what she believes. Your faith in God, your strength has always been an example to me. I've often wished for the same strength, the same ability to face problems head-on."

Nadine felt ashamed as he spoke. He was making her out to be so much better than she was. "Please, Clint. I'm not like that. I battled many times with God over my mother's illness. When she died I was relieved and had to ask God to forgive me that, as well."

"It doesn't matter, Nadine," he said quietly. "You have a beauty, a strength of character, a faith that has depth," he continued, his eyes on the hands that still played with her hair, as if unable to face her. "You're not the kind of person someone can get to know in one night, or one week, or month. You always intrigued me and scared me at the same time.''

What he said began a faint stirring in the depths of her being.

"I think I've always cared for you. I know I have,'' he amended. ''I don't know exactly how to say this except to be very honest.'' His hand stopped, resting on her shoulder, his finger caressing her neck. ''I love you, too, Nadine.''

She saw his lips move, heard the words as they settled into the empty, lonely part of her heart that she had kept blocked off for so long. As if in a daze, she slowly shook her head. ''What did you just say?''

''I said I love you.''

Nadine closed her eyes as if to hold the words in her mind. Words that echoed and resounded, drowning out so many other tiny voices that she had stored away—voices that had humiliated and hurt, sometimes unintentionally. She opened her eyes again and then, surprising herself at her audacity, reached over and pulled Clint's head down to hers.

Their lips met, seeking at first, then moving more slowly as pain was eased and loneliness filled. Finally Nadine pulled away, her heart as full as when she had first fully experienced God's love for her.

''I love you, too, Clint. I have loved you for years,'' she said simply, her hands resting on his shoulders, his clasped behind her waist.

He drew in a deep breath, as if he had been holding it since he first declared himself to her. "So that means if I ask you to marry me, you'll say yes?"

"More than likely," she returned.

He pulled her close once again and as she rested against his heart, she let her arms slip around him, enjoying the solidity of him.

"It worked, you know," she said softly, rubbing her cheek against his wrinkled shirt.

"What do you mean?"

"My life." Nadine tilted her head so she could look up at him. "It seemed so unorganized, like anything I started would end up going in a different direction. Yet God took all those scattered pieces and made them work."

Clint smiled down at her. "I know we can't expect a life without trouble, but I still choose the kind of marriage your parents had. Their faith and their love. They built on a strong foundation and I pray that we will, too."

And as Nadine returned his smile she sent up a prayer of thanks.

And then she stood on tiptoe and kissed her man.

Epilogue

Danielle Laidlaw snapped open the newspaper, turning first to the "Court Docket."

"Can you believe this, Leslie?" she asked in a shocked voice. "Eva Nedelof was caught shoplifting at the Red Rooster. Poor soul." Grandma Laidlaw clucked in dismay as she turned the page. The kitchen was silent except for the soft tick of the clock and the breathy sighs of Leslie's baby girl.

"Oh, my goodness." Danielle adjusted her reading glasses and leaned forward. "Listen to this headline. 'Skyline Contractors Files For Bankruptcy.'" She frowned as she read on, mouthing the words silently. "They are such a big company. What happened?"

"I heard they did a lot of work for that oil company that was starting up. The oil company went broke and took Skyline with them."

Danielle shook her head. "I always wondered why they didn't sue the paper like Nadine was so afraid they would after they ran that piece on Jake. Just goes to show you, 'Though the mills of God grind slowly, yet they grind exceeding small;/ Though with patience He stands waiting, with exactness grinds He all.' A German poet said that, and I agree.''

"When are Clint and Nadine supposed to be back from their honeymoon?" Leslie asked, shifting her daughter to her arm, changing the subject.

Danielle shrugged. "Nadine sounded anxious to come back. They've been gone for two weeks already."

"Who's running the paper?"

"Clint's uncle Dory came back for a while." Danielle pursed her lips. "How old is Dory Strepchuk?"

"Don't start, Grandma. According to Clint he's a confirmed bachelor."

"I did okay with Clint and Nadine."

"Clint had his eye on Nadine long before you came into the picture."

"How did you know?"

Leslie laughed at her grandmother's expression. "Don't pout, Grandma. I could see the way Clint looked at Nadine when he thought she wasn't looking."

"I could do quite well for Dory."

"Sounds like you have someone in mind." Leslie brushed a kiss across the top of her daughter's downy head.

"I do," Grandma said with a confident smile. "Me."

*   *   *   *   *

Dear Reader,

Whenever I tell a story, I start with my characters. What are their dreams, hopes and wishes? All of us have things that we want from life, yet prayerfully wonder if our motives are right.

Nadine wanted a number of things, but she had to learn to reevaluate her motives and her reasons for wanting them.

As we live our lives, our own wishes and dreams change with our situation. Sometimes we get what we want and then wish we hadn't. Sometimes we don't and are glad we didn't. I think the important thing is to remember that God uses all the good and bad things in our lives to shape and mold us, if we are willing.

I hope you enjoyed reading about Clint and Nadine. If you have any comments, I would love to hear from you. Please write me c/o Steeple Hill/Love Inspired, 300 East 42nd Street, New York, New York 10017.

Yours truly,

Carolyne Aarsen

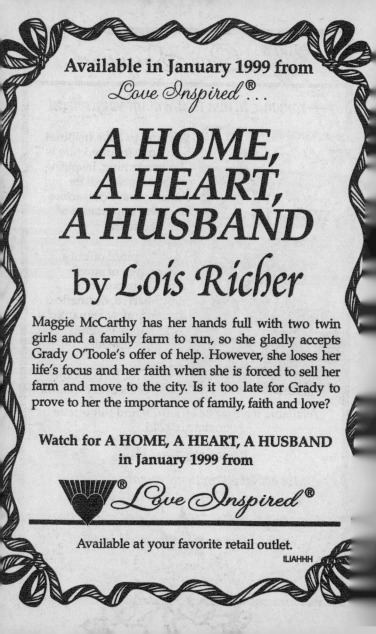

Available in February 1999 from
Love Inspired®...

WEDDING AT WILDWOOD

by *Lenora Worth*

When Isabel Landry returns to her hometown, she is forced to come to terms with the intolerance that forced her to abandon her dreams of being with the man she has always loved.

Watch for WEDDING AT WILDWOOD in February 1999 from

Love Inspired®

ILIWAW

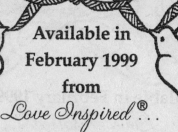